Infractions

Barbara Winkes

 ISBN: 978-1-0696671-0-6

Cover art by May Dawney Designs

For D.

Chapter One

J ordan held the front door open for Derek who was grateful to escape the downpour.

"You didn't have to come in person to tell us if the trip is off. If it rains like this all weekend…"

"Oh, no, the forecast is great for tomorrow and Sunday. This is an early gift from me and Kate." He held up the box in his hand. Jordan stepped back to let him inside, casting a perplexed look at her friend.

"We wanted to come by before the weekend, but there was no time," Derek said. "You need to think about baby-proofing the house—well, thanks to your observant friends, now you don't have to think about it anymore. This won't take long."

She followed him into the kitchen, taking out some paper towels to wipe the lid of the box, still speechless. She and Ellie had been packing for the trip earlier, thinking they'd see everyone the next day. This was a surprise.

"It's great, thank you…but you're aware that the baby isn't here yet, and even when she is, it will take some time before she can crawl?" Jordan was equally amused and touched by the gesture. The past few months had been challenging, and heartwarming—it seemed that their friends were almost as excited for the baby's arrival as she and Ellie were. That said a lot.

"There's nothing wrong with being prepared. You can focus on other things," Derek talked while he went around the room. "Besides, that's what Godparents do, right?"

"Well, I can't remember us discussing that yet...not that we need to."

Ellie was coming down the stairs, joining them in the kitchen.

"Anything I can get you?" she asked. "A beer..." She opened the fridge and peered inside. "Pickles—or cheesecake?"

Derek made a face at the last two options. "No, thanks."

"Yeah, I guess we'll pack that too, tomorrow. Those are essentials."

"So, you're all ready?"

"So ready," Jordan confirmed. "I can't wait."

"Good. It's a great place, you'll see. Casey and her husband will want to do some fishing, but you can take short walks or hang out by the lake."

Jordan's doctor had confirmed that she'd be fine heading out of the city with Ellie for a couple of days, as long as they took breaks during the drive. The cabins that belonged to an uncle of Derek's weren't exactly in the wild, just a little getaway with friends, the last one before the baby would arrive. A baby girl. They hadn't settled on a name yet.

"Doctor cleared it, right? You're not going to give birth up there?"

"Watch it," she warned. "That list of possible Godparents could still evolve...and no. Eight more weeks."

The thought filled her with terror or an out of bounds excitement—depending on the day.

"Wow. That time went by so quickly."

"Speak for yourself," Jordan said, laughing. She could have a sense of humor about it now, feeling tired, but mostly great in the recent months. Morning sickness had hit her hard, but that was over now, only certain smells making her nauseated. Another reason to escape the city for some fresh air.

She was looking forward to the company of her friends. Most of them worked active cases out in the field, while she'd been on light duty for some time. She had talked to Casey, who'd had her children while employed by the department, and browsed online groups to prepare. She didn't particularly love or hate those tasks that were always part of the job, but they had put her behind a desk for longer than she was used to. For a good reason, at least.

Something no one had warned her about was the habit of strangers to unleash uninvited comments and advice on a pregnant woman, the lack of respect for psychological and physical boundaries. Yes, getting away for a bit would be good for her, and Ellie, who was fiercely protective of her, too. Take a deep breath, relax.

A cabin full of cops, what could go wrong?

※

They would occupy two cabins—one for Jordan, Ellie, Derek and Kate, the other one for Casey Lyons and her husband, Detective Maria Doss and her girlfriend A.D.A. Esposito. The cabins each had a living area and kitchen, two bedrooms and one and a half baths, and a deck facing the lake. The drive was under two hours. Ellie had come up with a meticulous plan that included options for two to three breaks.

For once, the weather forecast had been right, and they parted to bright sunshine.

Derek hadn't been so wrong, Ellie reflected. The time was going by too damn fast. She was glad they had this opportunity.

Jordan, who had insisted on driving part of the way, had noticed her pensiveness.

"You're okay?" she asked softly. "You know the doc said it's all right."

"Of course. Just thinking. You remember Pauline asked if we wanted to have kids when you first brought me to dinner."

"Oh, yes, I remember. I'm so glad you didn't run away."

"And we almost adopted Ariel, and now, here we are."

Jordan waited, patiently, for her to form her thoughts.

"It's amazing. It's also...scary. Whatever we do, it's not just about us anymore." Ellie shook her head. "Really, don't listen to me. I don't know where that came from."

"It's fine. I feel the same way. A few years back I didn't even think this was possible. It wouldn't have been if I hadn't met you."

Ellie smiled, getting a little choked up like she often did lately. In the day-to-day life, a lot more had changed for Jordan than it had for her, and she kept reminding herself of that fact when she got all emotional about their future prospects. She loved her life, and what they were able to achieve together. If she hadn't shared some of her fears, about being good parents, teaching their child well so she would always respect herself and others...Perhaps now, only a few weeks away from Jordan giving birth, wasn't a good moment. Those fears never lingered for long anyway. Ellie knew what they were capable of. She had confidence in their relationship and their future parenting skills.

"Same here. I think you just missed the exit. You want to turn back, or can you make it to the next rest stop?"

Jordan sighed. "Let's go back. Better to be safe than sorry."

⁂

Her eyes went incredibly wide when she recognized him. He smiled, happy that she acknowledged him. She was trying to speak, but only garbled sounds made it past the gag.

"I think I can take that off in a moment," he thought out loud. "Please, don't waste your breath screaming. The next neighbors are too far away." He reached out to brush a hand over her hair. She flinched violently. "No, don't do that. I'm not going to hurt you. You are safe with me."

She didn't quite believe him yet, but he knew he had many ways to convince her. After all, true love was meant to be, wasn't it? She belonged with him, not that hippie husband of hers who probably did all the housework too. What could a woman want from a guy like that? He shook his head as if to underline his thought. She would understand eventually.

Carefully, he removed the gag, and as predicted, she started to scream.

"Help! Somebody help me!"

He sat across from her, waiting out her tantrum, smiling.

"What do you want from me?" She'd have to be careful, or that beautiful voice of hers would turn hoarse. He could never get enough of that voice.

"What is it that we all want?" That was better. If they were communicating, he was one step closer to making her understand her reality. She was his. "Love. I know this is all new for you, but I can be patient. In the meantime, I have enough love for both of us. You'll see."

"You are crazy!"

Even though he had expected that too, the remark stung.

"All I'm asking of you for now is to watch your language." He struggled to keep the anger out of his voice. "That's not so hard to do, is it? Right? Are you hungry?"

She gave him a blank stare. She was probably not going to admit it, but she had to be starving by now. Perhaps the drug he'd used made her a little sick in the beginning. She'd been awake for a while.

"Don't look so sad," he said. "We'll be happy together, I promise. Now let's have a little snack. I'll be right back."

Before he left the room, he made sure that she was still secured to the chair that was bolted to the floor. He had planned everything to the smallest detail. No more bad surprises.

Jordan was grateful for Ellie's planning—so far, the drive had been well over two hours, and those cabins were not yet in sight. The terrain was a bit higher up than they had expected. It would be fine, she told herself. She'd spent most of that time in a comfy chair on the deck anyway. Short walks on even ground. It didn't matter if they were a little farther away from the city than they'd imagined, because she was here to relax, not to give birth. Eight weeks, on the safe side.

Finally, a sign announced the property of Derek's uncle, and not much later, they saw a couple of familiar cars parked in front of one of two almost identical buildings. Derek had assured her they'd have the one with the slightly bigger full bathroom, for which she was grateful.

"Hey, look who finally found their way," Kate greeted them on the front deck. "Come on in."

Once inside, both Ellie and Jordan stood for a moment, in awe of the space. The build was classic log cabin, living room and kitchen updated and modern. Off to the side was a pool table.

"Yes, that was my reaction too," Kate said. "Derek's uncle is really cool for letting us stay here for free. All we have to do, he says, is leave the place exactly the way we found it. Shouldn't be too hard, should it?"

They all shared a laugh at that.

"All right, Valerie and Maria aren't here yet, but they should be soon. Take your time to get settled in."

Once the door was closed behind them, Ellie shook her head at the stunning mountain view and the décor worthy of a luxury hotel. Their room came with a king size bed, a sitting area, and a fireplace. "I had no idea it would be this amazing. This is perfect."

"It is," Jordan agreed. She went to the window, admiring the view, before she turned to Ellie and pulled her close. "Just how much time do you think they'll give us for settling in?"

Ellie laughed. "Not that much, I'm afraid. I think Maria and Valerie have arrived."

Chapter Two

After everyone had time to freshen up and put away clothes, Derek and Kate provided them with snacks and drinks. They would fire up the barbecue later in the evening. In between, most of them would check out the area around the cabins—both for enjoying nature, and because it was an indelible habit to check the perimeter, Jordan thought. For the moment, she was cozy and comfortable next to Ellie on the big couch, a glass of iced tea in hand, as Valerie Esposito detailed their adventures on the way.

"I had no idea you couldn't read a map," Maria Doss said affectionately.

"I can do it all right, I just didn't know you were this old-fashioned. There's something called GPS."

"It's good to discover those things early on in a relationship," Casey stated, sharing a smile with Jordan. "But you made it."

"Yes. Communication is key," Maria said. "I'm surprised though, this is higher up than we thought. You kept quite the secret from us."

Derek shrugged.

"Not really. Uncle Jackson only recently reconnected with my parents. He's been out of the country for long periods, but apparently, he bought this property years ago. The only downside is spotty cell phone reception."

"I don't mind. I could retire in a place like this," Casey said, and her husband nodded.

Jordan caught Ellie's gaze and shook her head. A weekend was great, but neither of them could imagine leaving the city and its own comforts for good—especially now, with the little one on the way.

She had balked at first, but finally she'd let him feed her the soup and some crackers. He sensed an air of anger from her, even more so than the fear. That was because she'd been misguided for such a big time of her life, not knowing what her place, her destiny was. Luckily, he'd found her, and many months after their paths had first crossed, he could now educate and guide her. The anger would dissipate. The fear would, eventually.

"I still don't understand," she said. "You say you love me. Why don't you give me some time then, until I'm ready, instead of locking me up here? If you love someone, you want them to choose you, right?"

He had to admire her, but things didn't work that way, not in the real world.

"I know what you need. It wouldn't be kind of me to withhold that from you, would it?"

"You're a freaking psychopath!" she yelled, startling them both. She stared at him, probably afraid of him snapping and hurting her. He had no such intention.

With a smile, he said, "Well, that's too bad. Look who just lost her bathroom privileges."

The sights of nature around them were breathtaking. Ellie and Jordan were the first ones to return to the cabin and its impressive deck. Being the hosts, Kate and Derek followed suit.

"Would you like a blanket? I could make you a tea?" Ellie offered.

"No, thank you, I'm fine." Fine was an understatement. She only hoped the baby would benefit from how relaxed she was in this environment and adopt more of that rather than her occasional frustrations over paperwork. She'd be the most Zen baby ever. Jordan smiled at her thoughts that inevitably revolved around her a lot of the time—all of the time—sometimes even during said paperwork.

"It's astonishing," Kate said, "You've all been here for a few hours, and there's been no shop talk. What am I missing?"

"I would like to say because it's quiet, but that's not true." Ellie sighed. "It's a bit of a miracle that we could all get away, but at least I could wrap up some court time before."

In the past few weeks, Jordan had accompanied her to court appointments when she had the time—which happened more often, because phone calls and reports could be done at different times. Most notably had been the conviction of Enid Montgomery, a woman in her early eighties who had murdered her friend, as well as her grand-nephew's parents. Jordan shuddered at the hateful stare the woman had given her. Enid, who had harbored bigoted and homophobic views all her life, knew that she was Ellie's wife, and she had been showing at the time. If she'd been superstitious, Jordan might have believed that the woman was trying to curse them.

That was a while ago, though, and she'd been working cases from a distance, phoning witnesses for interviews and such.

"Well, I'm glad you're here. Ellie, could I steal you for a second?" Kate asked.

It occurred to Jordan that Kate and Derek might have an announcement of their own, and that was the reason why they had invited them here.

⁂

"I could use a little help getting the stuff outside," Kate said, "but there's also something I wanted to tell you, and I wanted you to be the first to hear it."

"Oh my God, that's amazing! Congratulations!"

Ellie hugged her friend closely, only to realize that Kate was cracking up.

"Okay, back up a second, please. It's good news, but not that. Still not the plan. Okay, I'm sorry, I understand where you got the idea. You remember we spent some time with relatives of mine in Canada, sailing?"

"You mentioned that, yes," Ellie said, a tad flustered.

"We decided we wanted to get a boat! Take the next few months practicing and saving up...Now that Jordan will be on maternity leave soon, Derek plans to do some more overtime, and I got an internship—it's going to be amazing!"

"Well, then—congratulations!"

Ellie marveled once again at the fact how different their respective life goals had become. In the years they had known each other, plans had been made and crossed out, sometimes by forces outside of their power. But they had never given up. When Ellie came back from the travels she'd gone on after the death of her parents, when staying wouldn't be enough to deal with the grief, she had known what she wanted out of life. And later, after meeting Jordan, those goals had become crystal clear.

Kate had come back from an incredible loss, now happy, married to Jordan's partner, and they were going to buy a boat—what was not to celebrate about that?

"I bought some alcohol-free sparkling wine," Kate said. "We tried it. It's pretty good."

It was A.D.A. Esposito who later brought the subject back to Montgomery. It was a case very much unlike any of them had seen in their careers, a murder solved this long after the fact.

"Can you imagine hating yourself this much that you kill people, just for the appearance of what you think is normal? I'd feel sad for her if she wasn't such a cold-blooded criminal."

"Sad is not the right word," Jordan said. "For sure, she would have had problems coming out as a young woman, but others faced the same prejudice. Without killing anyone."

"Did anyone ever give you guys crap growing up?"

Jordan and Valerie had had a brief affair, years before Ellie, too short to ever address subjects like that—or for Jordan to tell her the truth. She'd faced some challenges in her youth, though homophobia hadn't been the biggest. Even later, she'd only heard a handful uninvited and misinformed comments from suspects, like the members of the cult they'd dismantled. Lucky.

"I heard a few stupid 'jokes,' usually when people didn't know. In middle school, a girl once told me her parents didn't want me over anymore," Ellie recalled. "Mom went over and gave them a piece of her mind, though it was pretty clear I wouldn't go to that house again."

Casey shook her head. "I don't get parents who raise their kids that way, to become close-minded bigots. What kind of life is that?"

Her question hung in the room unanswered. Maria Doss pushed back her chair and picked up her beer bottle.

"I don't know about you, but I'd like to make use of that pool table before we leave. Who's with me?"

Ellie, Kate and Jeff, Casey's husband, got up as well and joined her on the other side of the room. Valerie took the moment to leave for the bathroom.

Jordan remained at the table with the rest of their group. Casey cast a thoughtful look after Maria. "Speaking of coming out, I don't want to be the clueless straight person in the room, but weren't you two dating at some point?"

"Sure. I knew," Derek said with a shrug. "Don't look at me like that. It wasn't for me to tell."

They changed the subject before Valerie returned, but Jordan couldn't help thinking it was good to have friends who could keep a secret.

Friends. Godparents.

Valerie had made a beeline for her and Maria's room to get a deck of cards.

"You're all in for a round of poker?"

"Not me," Casey said. "I'm not on a detective's salary."

"We'll have a lot of expenses coming, so I don't think it's a good idea," Jordan added.

Valerie shook her head with a laugh. "You guys are hilarious, I was going to start with quarters. Besides, you might win yourself a baby wardrobe. And speaking of which, have you thought of a name yet?"

"Not really. We might make the names of my and Ellie's mom a part of it."

"That's a great idea," Casey acknowledged.

It might be hormones making her emotional, but Jordan felt deeply grateful for the people around her. It had taken her a while to open up to them. They knew her well enough to understand that when she was talking about her mother, she'd always mean Pauline Carpenter first. And no one would criticize her for it.

"Yeah, I think we'll go with something like that."

"If you can't make up your mind, how about naming her after your good friend?" Valerie suggested. "Okay, you don't have to. Are we going to play or not?"

"I'm in. That boat's not going to come cheap. Come on, Jordan. You used to be good at this," Derek said.

"That was a long time ago. I'm rusty...but...okay."

Casey lifted her hands in defeat. "I'm going to regret this. Let's do it."

No one had gone into debt at the pool or poker table. Ellie's last concerns about the weekend away from home had disappeared when they excused themselves to curl up under the sheets in the amazingly comfortable bed. She had wanted to stay awake a bit longer knowing that Jordan had increasing trouble to get comfortable at night. The fresh air and fairly long day made her fall asleep moments after her head hit the pillow. Sometime that night, she dreamed that the rain had come back, getting heavier and heavier as it pounded against the window, until Ellie thought it might break the glass...

She jolted awake to realize the sound was real, but it wasn't rain. Someone was knocking on the front door like they were trying to break it down.

"Help! I need help, please, open the door!"

She reached for her clothes, realizing that Jordan was already wearing pants and a sweater.

"You stay here," Ellie said. "I'm going to check it out."

Jordan's expression told her that she wasn't completely on board with the idea but simply acknowledged that there was a reason for it. In the main room, she ran into Derek who was also heading for the door from which the insistent knocking came. There was no new car, so whoever was out there must have come on foot? Raindrops on the window showed her that the rain had indeed come back.

Derek yanked the door open to reveal a man who was shaking and crying. His shirt stuck to his chest with sweat, his hands...damn. There was no mistaking the copper smell.

"What happened?" she asked. "Are you hurt?"

"No, not me. It's my girlfriend. You need to help her!"

"Where are you?" Ellie remembered that during their walk, they had only seen a couple of other buildings from afar. Had the couple been camping somewhere in the area?

Casey and Maria came through the open front door, and Jordan had joined them as well.

"We are spending the weekend up here, Betty and I. She fell. It was a terrible accident," the man cried. "Please, I don't have cell phone service, and I didn't know what to do."

Ellie shared a startled look with Maria. Leaving a loved one like this was a terrible choice to make, but if she was seriously hurt, he probably didn't dare move her.

"We'll come with you," she said.

"I'll join you," Derek added.

"No, we'll be fine." Ellie hoped to convey without words that she'd prefer for him to start his Godfatherly duties *now*. It wasn't just that she wanted Jordan to stay here, though Ellie did prefer that solution. Someone would have to alert the local authorities. Last time she'd checked, cell phone reception had been spotty but better closer to the road. "You guys call 911. The address?" she asked the distraught man.

"It's a couple of miles East. I'll show you. Please hurry. I tried to make her comfortable, but...I don't know..."

"Let's go," Ellie said. "What's your name?"

"Robert Hogan."

"Okay, Robert. We'll try to help Betty, I promise."

As they headed out in the dark, with the man in tow, she suppressed a shudder, the feel that she was still caught in a dream. She hoped there would be a happy ending to this abrupt invasion of their weekend getaway.

⁓

They didn't get service anywhere around the house.

"All of a sudden, detaching from everything is not so relaxing after all," Casey remarked.

Jordan agreed with her, though she had to admit, for a selfish moment, she was only grateful that it wasn't time for her to give birth yet. When closer to her due date, there was no way she'd go outside a certain radius around the hospital.

But they had to do something, find a place where they could call for an ambulance. Something told her that they'd need the local police on the scene in case this didn't end well. There had been a lot of blood on the man's hands.

"There was a bar somewhere close," Derek recalled. "They must have a landline."

"Sure, that's worth a try. Let's go find it."

He cast Jordan an incredulous glance.

"What? It's just driving around. Besides, if I correctly interpreted the non-verbal communication you had with Ellie earlier, she wants you to stay close. There's no time to argue."

An easy win.

"Something you want to tell me?" he asked once they were in the car. There was something, actually. Jordan knew she could always count on him to give a frank impression.

"More like ask you. You saw what I saw, right? This guy...he seemed a bit over the top."

"Well, his girlfriend was hurt, potentially fatally. I understand him freaking out."

"Yeah."

"What does that mean?"

"It means I know I can't keep Ellie from doing the job, and what's necessary, but I'm glad that both she and Maria have guns."

"There is that."

Jordan admitted to herself that she'd hoped he might tell her she was overreacting. They both knew that Robert Hogan might not have told them the truth. Even if he had, the implications were disturbing.

After driving the winding roads for about five minutes, they saw a light.

"That's it," Derek said. "Let's hope this works out."

Jordan had the urge to whisper to the baby, to explain the situation to her as she often did now when she was alone, or with no one but Ellie around. No matter how well Derek could guard a secret, she held back the impulse.

Chapter Three

Hogan's cabin was a bit smaller than the property of Derek's uncle but had a similar layout. All the lights were on inside. Hogan had obviously left in a hurry. The scenery could have been cozy, if it wasn't for the blood smears on the floor. Ellie stepped closer to the couch while Maria kept an eye on Hogan.

The woman, Betty, had suffered a severe head wound, blood seeping through the towel he had put on her head, into the pillow below. He had covered her with a blanket. A fire was dying down in the fireplace. Ellie stepped back, feeling defeated.

The woman's eyes were staring into nothing. She leaned down to check for a pulse anyway, receiving confirmation for what she already knew.

"You can help her, right? Your friends will call an ambulance, and they will save her. They must save her!"

His voice rose to something akin to a scream. Ellie turned to him.

"I'm so sorry," she said.

"No!" He fell to his knees next to the couch. "This isn't true! Do something!"

"I'm sorry, Robert," Ellie repeated. "She's gone."

"No!" With one abrupt move, he swept the dishes, two glasses and plates with utensils, off the table.

"Let's go outside," Maria said, her tone calm and firm. "Tell us what happened, while we wait for the police."

"Police?" He seemed shocked but followed them outside onto the deck. "Why? This was an accident! She fell on the stairs outside and hit her head."

"You saw it happen?" Like Maria, Ellie wanted to be cautious. If his story was true, it was incredibly tragic—if. The couple might have had a fight, and she was running away in anger. Or, he had pushed her in anger. Did he mean for her to get hurt? That was something the locals would have to find out.

"No, I didn't. I don't know why she went out in the middle of the night. I didn't hear anything. I woke up and she wasn't there, so I went looking for her...then I found her there."

He pointed to the stairs leading down to the parking area. Ellie could see the dark stains on the wood. That had to have been a horrific fall. Her stomach churned at the images her mind produced.

"What did you do?" Maria asked in the same calm tone.

"I helped her get up and into the cabin. She was in a lot of pain, confused. I covered her and tried to stop the bleeding. It wouldn't stop!"

"For how long do you think you tried?" Ellie inquired.

"What are you saying? I had to do something, she was bleeding so much! I knew that there were other cabins around here, so I went to get help. I didn't know she was hurt this badly." He covered his face with his hands, tears smearing the dried blood. "Oh God, Betty. I can't lose her!"

"Robert. Please, think for a moment. Did she say anything to you? Could there have been another person?"

"I don't know!" he sobbed.

Ellie and Maria shared another look, before Ellie turned her gaze back to the blood on the stairs, remembering the smears inside. That much blood was consistent with the woman's head wound, and still—if she'd been able to stand on her feet, it seemed that the pattern should be a different one.

She hoped Jordan and their friends would be able to contact 911. The local authorities would take it from here.

At least she could be assured that Jordan was safe back in the cabin.

She didn't trust Hogan.

Jordan couldn't believe what she was seeing.

"I think I'm still dreaming," she said, and Derek didn't argue with her assessment. They had found the bar he'd seen earlier, but unlike his uncle's luxury accommodations, this building looked run down. Several motorcycles were parked outside, and they could hear the laughter from its rowdy patrons. "That's...interesting," she added.

"Yeah. I'm glad Ellie isn't seeing this. She wouldn't be happy I took you here. I'll risk sounding patronizing, but I'd like you to wait in the car."

"No way. If you think it's not safe inside, I'm not going to stay in the car by myself. It's a bunch of loud and drunk people in a bar. Besides, we're not here to arrest anyone. All we need is a phone."

Derek wasn't entirely convinced.

"I'm beginning to think I'll regret ever suggesting this trip. Okay, let's do this quick."

The music still played on, but the sound level dropped considerably, conversations coming to a halt when they walked inside, looks following them all the way from the entrance to the bar. Some intrigued, some hostile, all more invasive than she liked. Okay, so maybe Derek had a point when he wanted her to stay at the cabin. She was tired, the smells—greasy food, booze, sweat—making her nauseated. Quick, in, out. Ellie never had to learn details about the place.

She could only imagine what some of them were thinking.

The bartender gave them the once over.

"You lost?" he asked, barely able to keep the grin off his face. Jordan had met a few bikers over the years, and she knew not to stereotype. Those of the particular brand present in this bar didn't return the favor.

"Man, I don't think I can help you with the mess you got yourself into there." Two men sitting a few stools away laughed so hard one of them almost fell off his.

"Charming," Jordan said and slammed her badge onto the counter. She might have to spray it with a disinfectant later. "We need to use your phone. There's been an accident in one of the cabins, and we need an ambulance there now. You have a landline?"

"Sure. You can put that away. We're always happy to help. You want to come with me?"

They followed him into a messy-looking office space.

"There you go, help yourself." He stayed, leaning against the wall. Derek picked up the phone and made the call, providing dispatch with the address Hogan had given them, and as many details as they had at this moment. He also gave the address of his uncle's cabin so the local cops could reach them later.

As they were leaving, Jordan heard the inevitable comments combining racist and sexist sentiment from patrons.

"Let it go," Derek muttered.

"Just this time. Assholes."

When they were back in the car, both of them breathed a sigh of relief. Jordan found a packet of wet wipes in her pocket, of which she handed one to Derek.

"I take solace in the fact that some of them will catch something from this place. Wow. I did not expect that."

"Neither did I," Derek admitted. "Let's go back now."

The local sheriff arrived with his deputy, the latter looking like he was barely legal. Ellie felt for him when he blanched spectacularly at the sight of the woman's body.

"I'm glad you're here," she said. "I assume you spoke to Detective Henderson? My friends went to a bar close by to make a call because we couldn't get a signal."

"The bar. Right."

The sheriff and his deputy exchanged a glance which Ellie didn't know how to interpret. They had more urgent matters to address.

"We need to contact the medical examiner," she said, lowering her voice even though Hogan was far out of earshot. "We haven't had a chance yet to take a look at the other rooms. Mr. Hogan says it was an accident, but I feel like there's something he isn't telling us."

"Lady, relax, I think we can take it from here."

"I'm Detective Harding. This is Detective Doss, Homicide."

"Oh yes, the dispatch officer mentioned something," the sheriff said, a tad flustered. "You guys are having a weekend outing up here? Bad timing, I'd say."

Ellie wasn't interested in making small talk. "There were dishes on the table. I don't know, maybe they had an argument or something. You've seen those blood smears on the floor? He says he helped her walk to the couch."

Sheriff Watkins looked over to where Hogan was standing with Maria Doss and the deputy.

"Poor fellow might be confused, but we'll check for that. I think you can get back to your vacation. We'll have an investigator from the county over if necessary. Thank you. We'll wait for the coroner and take Mr. Hogan to the station to ask a few more questions. If we need anything from you, we'll know where to find you. It's late. We got this," he emphasized when Ellie was about to follow him into the room behind the first door.

She ignored him and went inside.

"Detective! That's not necessary. You're out of your jurisdiction."

"I'll be gone in a few minutes," she promised.

The master bedroom and bath showed nothing out of the ordinary. Clothes and toiletries for both of the cabin's occupants. In the hallway, she saw a trap door in the ceiling. "What's behind this?" Ellie asked, pointing up.

"You thought we'd forget to check?" Sarcasm she could handle. At least he wasn't trying to deter her any longer. He went ahead and pulled the chain that brought down the folded stairs. "There you go, Ma'am. After you."

Clearly, he hoped to have her and Maria out of here soon. Ellie would be just as happy to leave, but first she wanted to know what was up there.

When she found the light switch, the single light bulb illuminated some furniture covered with drapes, and boxes filled with books, magazines and a few records. Nothing out of the ordinary, or particularly disturbing. Taking a step backwards, she suppressed a curse when her hip collided with the back of a chair.

The chair didn't move.

"Everything all right up there?" the sheriff called.

"Yes, I'm fine." She removed the sheet, then kicked the chair slightly. It stayed in place. Crouching down, Ellie realized it was bolted to the floor.

"Sheriff, come here for a second?"

"What is it?"

She pointed to her finding. "That's out of the ordinary, don't you think? You should have your team take a look when they're done downstairs."

"Because of that chair?" He looked doubtful.

"Yes, because of that chair. Are you going to make those calls?"

He grumbled something as he went back down, but a moment later, he was on the phone. Ellie gave the room a cursory search before she climbed down the stairs as well.

⁕

While Sheriff Watkins was talking to his deputy, she took a moment to check her phone. Seeing a couple of bars, Ellie hurried to call Jordan before they'd disappear again.

"Hey, I just wanted to let you know Maria and I are okay, but his girlfriend...It was already too late when we arrived."

"I'm sorry. Thank you for calling though."

"I suppose all went okay on your side."

"Yes, no problems. When are you coming back?...Ellie?"

The signal was starting to fade in and out.

"I'm here. We're about to wrap up. I don't think they'll need or want us to be here for the rest—but don't wait up for me. You were supposed to get some rest."

Jordan laughed wryly. "I'm not sure that's going to happen, but I'll try. See you later."

"See you." Ellie wasn't sure if Jordan had heard her as the connection was gone altogether.

It was close to 2:30 when they arrived back at the cabin, and Ellie could finally crawl into bed next to Jordan, snuggling into her embrace.

⁕

A little after seven a.m. they sat around the big dining table for breakfast, trying to figure out what happened a few hours ago, only a couple of miles away. Sheriff Watkins had made it clear that they would work with the county and were well equipped to take care of the situation.

It seemed like there was nothing out of the ordinary in the rooms of Hogan's cabin, yet Ellie had left with the nagging feeling that they'd overlooked something. Those blood smears were haunting her. And that chair in the attic.

"We can all come up with the wildest theories," Valerie Esposito remarked. "That doesn't make them true. People do strange things in a traumatic situation. The chair might have been there for a long time. On the other hand, people do terrible things to one another."

"I think he dragged her back inside. That doesn't mean he meant to kill her...but it's odd. If it wasn't him...was someone else there?"

She saw Derek and Jordan exchange a look she wasn't sure how to interpret.

"The sheriff and his deputy gave me strange looks when they said where you called from. Why is that? That bar, what did it look like?"

Another one of those looks passed between the partners, doing nothing to reassure Ellie.

"All right. Anything you aren't telling me?"

"This is not our job," Derek said. "It's puzzling, yes, and it certainly messed with our vacation, but they will take care of it."

Ellie glared at him, surprised that it did have any effect.

"Biker hangout," he added. "Not the friendly kind either, but once they knew we were cops, they refrained to verbal BS."

"Jesus, and you're telling me this now?"

Jordan sighed.

"We made the call, we came back here. There was nothing to tell."

"I can't believe you." Ellie shook her head, then got up and served herself from the coffee pot. "Sorry, I need some caffeine. This is...I don't even know what to say."

"Well, we didn't know it was that bad, and it was the only place to get to a landline. Relax," Jordan implored. "It's over."

"Yeah. I guess."

"Anyone still wants to go fishing?" Casey asked dryly.

Ellie took a deep breath and sat back down. She might have overreacted, but she was still disturbed by the image of the woman who had died on that couch, all alone—and the idea that Derek and Jordan had gone inside that place knowing it could be dangerous.

She had to admit that she could understand Jordan much better now for acting in a way she had at times found overprotective, bordering on overbearing. But things were different. She knew Jordan was a tad bored on light duty, but she didn't have to jump at an occasion like this, did she?

"I think we're going to drive home after lunch," Valerie said. "It might be outside our jurisdiction, but I'm going to have a hard time relaxing, under the circumstances."

Kate looked sad. Ellie couldn't come up with anything to reassure her friend.

"Yeah, I know what you mean."

❦

"You know I would never do anything to harm her," Jordan said when they were on their way home, and Ellie had barely spoken in half an hour. "It was just about making that call. Driving around for a few minutes, it wasn't bad for the baby."

"I know."

"It's out of our hands now."

"I know."

"But?" Jordan prompted.

"I'm not sure," Ellie admitted. "I might be getting a little paranoid. You're the one who's pregnant, but it seems like my emotions are all over the place, and I don't know why. You've done so great."

Jordan seemed just as startled as she was to realize she was close to tears.

"Well, the toughest part is yet to come. Besides, you've been great too, working a full-time job and being there for me every step of the way. I'm not taking that for granted. I'll never take you for granted."

"I know that. I'm sorry. Wow." Ellie took a deep breath. So much for her decision not to share any of her own fears. "That was so unexpected. If it was an accident like he said, he just lost the love of his life. If he intended it...Was she in an abusive relationship, or did he trick her into coming up here somehow? No matter how you look at it, it's a terrible story."

"Yeah, I get you. The fact that there are so many unanswered questions doesn't make it any easier. Damn, what a world. Makes me wonder if we should homeschool our daughter and while we're at it, never let her out until she's thirty or so."

Jordan cracked up laughing at Ellie's expression.

"I guess we'll find other ways, then."

"I'm sure she'd prefer that."

"Yeah. We haven't even settled on a name yet."

"The subject came up briefly while you were playing pool," Jordan remembered. "We thought about this before, naming her after our moms? Meredith Pauline?"

"You'd be okay with that?"

At this moment, Ellie was certain she was experiencing sympathetic pregnancy syndrome. Whatever the reason for her being this emotional, she was glad not to be driving.

"Of course. Meredith Pauline Carpenter Harding." Jordan chuckled. "Is she going to hate us?"

"How about we shorten it to Meri? And I won't feel left out if it's just Carpenter. You're doing the hard part."

At the next red light, Jordan took her hand, and just like that, they had a plan. Ellie could breathe a lot easier.

Chapter Four

"**G**ood morning."

"Ellie, hi. I heard you had an interesting weekend," Detective Rogers said as he held the door to the break room open for her.

"Thanks. That's quite the understatement. New case?" she asked with regard to the thin file he was holding.

"Oh yeah, I was just going to get some coffee for me and the husband. Strange story. Woman plans to have a weekend with a friend, so he goes away with a few buddies, comes back to realize the wife never made it to her friend's."

"They didn't communicate the whole time?"

He shrugged. "I don't get it either, but apparently it was something they did often. He went fishing, no cell phone service for some of the time—when he checked his messages again, he realized he had a dozen or so. Anyway, I have to go back."

"Sure. See you."

As he juggled the file and both coffees, a photograph fell out of the folder. Ellie bent down to pick it up and froze.

"Crap," she said. "I think I just solved your case."

It took only a few minutes of coordination to realize that Betty was Elizabeth Randall, reported missing by her husband Matt. He was in shock, angry, but when Ellie joined Rogers in the interview room, Randall wasn't hesitant to talk.

"I've never heard of a Robert Hogan. What kind of crap is that? Why was she with him?"

Ellie would have liked to know. This changed everything. The Randalls lived in a townhouse not far from her in-laws, Jack and Pauline. Robert Hogan would have to answer many more questions, and he'd have to answer them here.

She was still questioning the husband's statement about how late he had discovered Elizabeth's disappearance, but between the two of them, she found Hogan a whole lot more suspicious.

"Mr. Randall...I know this is hard, but I have to ask."

"You want to know if Liz was having an affair?" he cut her off. "No. That's not possible. She would never do that to me. We were happy!" He, too, was crying.

Ellie remembered Robert Hogan, sobbing, yelling at them to save her. How did he know Elizabeth Randall in the first place?

"I'm so sorry for your loss," she said. "I promise you we'll find out the truth."

She couldn't detect anything in his gaze to tell her he might be threatened by that promise.

After an officer had walked Randall out, Ellie turned to Rogers.

"Let's go find Hogan."

※

"Could you do me a favor?" Ellie asked when she stopped by Jordan's desk. "Actually, I need two," she corrected herself. She looked excited. Even if they hadn't been at work, and the question was basically a technicality, Jordan wouldn't have been able to tell her no. It should come at no surprise to her, not anymore, but sometimes she was still secretly thrilled about the way Ellie had made herself at home in her career. Even when it meant that their roles were reversed sometimes.

"Sure. What do you need?"

"About the woman who died Saturday night...Her husband just reported her missing."

Ellie quickly brought her up to speed.

"The friend, Marcia Loman, will be here in a minute. Could you do the interview with her? If you have time, could you also see if you can find an address for Hogan other than the cabin. The Randalls own a townhouse in the city, and I'm thinking he might have an address around close by."

"Makes sense," Jordan agreed. "I'll get on it."

Normally, that would be her, going after Hogan and asking the questions, but one, Ellie was perfectly capable, and two...Jordan knew it would have been the better choice to stay in the cabin. Lesson learned.

She went to check for an empty interview room she could use later and then ran a search on Robert Hogan. As expected, there were a little over half a dozen.

Let the fun begin.

Jordan had ruled out five of them by the time Marcia Loman arrived. Jordan got up to greet her and suppressed a sigh at the woman doing a double take. Was the concept of a pregnant cop really that startling to people?

In the interview room, Marcia Loman confirmed that the Randalls' marriage was a happy one.

"They spent time with their respective friends, so what? Liz wasn't really into fishing, and Matt sure didn't want to join us for a pedicure...but they were happy, truly happy. The real deal that you get jealous of, but you can't blame them, because

33

they're so adorable at the same time..." Marcia's eyes welled up, tears starting to stream down her face as she seemed to only now realize the finality of the recent events.

Jordan couldn't blame her.

"I'm sorry. I know this is painful, but we need to find out why Elizabeth was in that cabin. Did you ever hear her talk about a Robert Hogan?"

"No, never," Marcia answered right away. "Is that him? The one who murdered her?"

"We don't know yet. You're certain she never mentioned that name? Bob maybe? Anyone she met recently?"

"No. Liz wasn't a cheater."

Jordan noticed that both the husband and friend called her Liz, while Betty was the name Hogan had used for her. Had she led a double life—or had he taken her against her will? That explanation was starting to make more and more sense—but why did he call for help rather than dispose of the body? Nothing much would have pointed to him as the killer, at least from what she could see so far. Why take the risk? Of course, some murderers liked to test the boundaries of what they could get away with. She didn't think he knew he'd find cops next door, people who'd notice the holes in his story pretty much right away.

"Okay. Did you observe anything strange lately? Like changes in her behavior, or someone following her around?"

"Lately, no." Her eyes went wide, and Jordan instantly knew she had touched on something.

"It's probably nothing."

"Please, tell me."

"It was long ago, anyway. Liz and Matt moved here about two years ago, to be closer to his family. She once told me that in the old home, she used to have a strange feeling, like someone was watching her...I can't imagine it has anything to do with this.

She said it was a spooky house, outside the city, and she was glad when she and Matt moved here."

It might have been just her imagination, but in Jordan's experience, when a woman's instinct told her something was wrong, she was probably right to assume that—especially considering what happened to her.

"What about former relationships, did she talk to you about any?"

"Not really. She and Matt were high school sweethearts, married right out of college."

"Do you have an address for their old house?"

"No, I'm sorry. I'm sure Matt can help you with that. Liz said it was about fifty miles from here."

"Okay. Thank you. If you can think of anything else, please don't hesitate to call."

Jordan jotted down some notes to brief Ellie on later and, after Marcia Loman had left, she settled down for more research.

Sheriff Watkins had agreed to meet Ellie at the small police station, but when she arrived, he wasn't available, out on an emergency. She waited for a while, then recognized the deputy she'd seen the other day rushing by.

"Hi!" She jumped to her feet. "I'm here to see Sheriff Watkins about Mr. Hogan..."

"Didn't you hear?" he asked, surprised. "The sheriff is up at Hogan's cabin. Someone torched it last night."

"What? Was anyone hurt?"

"No, but Sheriff Watkins is with Mr. Hogan at the cabin right now. Well, what's left of it. If you hurry up, you can probably catch them."

You could have told me right away, Ellie thought, but she didn't voice her irritation. "Can you tell me anything about the state of the investigation? It's in our hands now. Mrs. Randall was reported missing by her husband."

"Again, I'd like to advise you to talk to Sheriff Watkins."

"Thanks anyway," she muttered and left. Back in her car, she pulled out of the parking lot and took the route to Hogan's cabin, past the property of Derek's uncle. She wanted to ask about any possible leads from the bar as well, but it didn't look like she'd get anything out of the deputy. With a little luck, she'd find out what she needed from both Watkins and Hogan. The latter, she wanted to talk to in an interrogation room. Ellie hoped he'd see the urgency even before she could get a warrant.

⁂

"I don't even know where to start...Betty...and now I have to deal with this." It occurred to her that whenever she met Hogan, he was crying. It never seemed to feel like honest emotion, more like something he thought they'd expect.

"You're going to investigate this, right? I'm sure one of those bikers did it. They once gave us the evil eye." He stared at her intently. "You don't think one of them killed her that night? Oh my God."

He'd told them she'd been confused, in pain. He'd never answered their questions about a possible third person before, and the present moment seemed a bit too convenient. Ellie made a mental note of this yet another discrepancy. The bar was a few minutes by car away from Hogan's cabin.

"Mr. Hogan, I know you already talked to the Sheriff's office, but there are a few more questions regarding Betty." She purposefully didn't use the woman's full name. "I need you to come with me to the department so we can sort this out."

"Yes, I understand. Can I follow you in my car?" He turned back to what was now a pile of smoldering timber. "I guess the local police will be here for a while—again."

"Yes, please. Thank you."

As soon as Ellie was within reach of cell phone service, she called A.D.A. Esposito to ask her to be present. She had a feeling.

⁂

Jordan was quite sure she had found the right Robert Hogan, registered at 36 River Street, three blocks away from the Randalls' townhouse. She had also found the Randalls' former address. As she was putting everything in order, Valerie Esposito walked in, her coffee to go in hand.

"Oh, hey. Is Ellie back already?"

"Not yet. Can I help you?"

"She wanted me to sit in for an interview. Would you mind if I wait with you? Wow." Valerie didn't wait for an answer. "This vacation took a strange turn, didn't it? Did you hear that the guy's cabin burned? Ellie just told me. They're suspecting arson."

"No. So he's in hiding?"

"Actually no, it gets stranger from here. He's the one coming in for the interview."

"Strange indeed. All right. You might want to take a look at this."

Valerie whistled when she realized what the papers Jordan was showing her, meant.

"Now that's interesting. It would be quite the coincidence if they lived this close and never met."

"That's what I'm thinking. Doesn't tell us if she went freely or not, though."

"Yeah, that's what Ellie hopes to find out. And here they are."

Valerie picked up her coffee when she saw Ellie and Hogan heading for the interview room, Ellie signaling for her to follow.

"You want to watch with me?" she asked Jordan who got to her feet as quickly as she was capable.

"Sure."

After finishing up the formalities of the interview, Ellie sat across from Robert Hogan. She found it astonishing that he didn't seem much concerned about the setting. Then again, he might be innocent. Elizabeth Randall's death could be a tragic accident, but it was becoming less and less likely.

With the cabin, any possible evidence had burned as well. But there were pictures of those smears. The autopsy would be done here, by their own M.E. All ducks in a row. Knowing what was going to happen next, and that the case was in their own precinct now, was a relief.

"Mr. Hogan, you called Betty your girlfriend. When did you first meet her?"

"I told that to the sheriff already. Look, I really want to help, but I hope I didn't drive all the way here for nothing."

"I don't think you did. Every little detail matters."

"We met in a supermarket...about eighteen months ago. You want the address?"

The question had a bit of a sarcastic tone to it.

"Yes, please," Ellie said.

"Whatever. It was love at first sight."

"You knew that she was married?"

"Married? No, she didn't tell me." He hesitated. "Well...I assume there was a reason for that? Did you check on the husband? Maybe he killed her."

"How? He was on a trip with friends. Remember you told us her fall was an accident? Then, that it might have been one of the bikers? How did you come to that conclusion? Why do you think someone killed her?"

He raked a hand through his hair.

"I don't know, okay? I'm not sure of anything. A few days ago, I had a life, a relationship, a home—it's all gone now!"

There was a knock on the door, and Jordan came in.

"Sorry to interrupt."

Ellie caught the gaze Hogan gave her, wholeheartedly understanding the frustration Jordan harbored lately. Too many men already believed that women's bodies belonged to them, but for even more people, the bodies of pregnant women belonged to everybody.

"Yeah, why don't we take a break? Would you like me to bring you anything, Mr. Hogan? Water, or a coffee?"

He finally tore his gaze away to look back at Ellie.

"No, thank you, Detective. I want to get this over with. I need to find a hotel room. As you know, my place went up in flames."

"Yes, about that. It's a good thing that we got a crime scene unit into the place before that happened, right?"

"I'm not sure what you're trying to imply, Detective. Betty came to spend the weekend with me."

"Okay. I'm sure you cleared that with Sheriff Watkins already, but I'm curious. Why was that chair in the attic bolted down? What was that for?"

"It was like that when I bought the place. All the furniture upstairs, those records, I'd never gotten around to clearing it out. Well, too late for that now."

"It is." Ellie pushed back her chair and got up. "Will you excuse me for a moment? I'll be right back."

"He's not budging." Ellie sighed as she joined Jordan and Valerie in the observation area. "I'm going to confront him with what you found, next, but I'm not hopeful."

"You're on the right track," Valerie assured her.

Jordan nodded. "He might have cleaned up the attic before he came to us...but it's hard to remove every single trace. We'll know more after the autopsy too. You're doing good."

"All right, thanks for the vote of confidence. I have to get back in there."

Jordan patted her shoulder lightly.

"You got this. Go."

Valerie's indulgent smile didn't bother Ellie one bit. She stepped back into the room and sat back across from Hogan.

"All right, Mr. Hogan. You said you needed to find a room—is there any reason why you can't go to your apartment? The one that's only a few steps away from where Elizabeth Randall lived with her husband?"

He held her gaze, unfazed.

"No, I can't go back there. I sublet it a while ago to save up some money. I was staying in the cabin...obviously that's not an option any longer."

"Mr. Hogan, have you ever lived in Caton?"

"Why do you want to know?"

"In fact, has Park Street in Caton ever been your address?"

"What is this all about? Yes, I lived in Caton."

"Where you were the Randalls' next-door neighbor. And you never talked to Elizabeth? Didn't realize she lived there with her husband? You must admit, none of this makes sense. Maybe you actually had feelings for her, but she didn't return them. Two years, or longer, that's quite some time. You got angry."

"No, no, no, you're making this all up. I want my lawyer now."

40

"You can call him from here, of course. So, you admit you knew Elizabeth back in Caton?"

"I'm not admitting anything. I want to call her right now!"

"Of course." Ellie got to her feet. "Please, follow me."

Chapter Five

E llie was on the phone with the sheriff's office to see if they had found anything at the site of the burned down cabin that could help. Like everyone who had witnessed the interview, she didn't buy Hogan's evasions, but unfortunately, what they had wouldn't be enough to hold him for long. He had come forward, first after the incident, now he had come to the station freely...It wasn't solid enough yet, and Valerie had confirmed it before she left.

Nevertheless, Jordan thought the biker angle should be something to check out, not that anyone would let her go back to the bar. Not that she wanted to if she was honest, but she had someone on her mind who might be able to help. For sure, they needed to ask some more questions around there. Someone might have seen something, and given the men's behavior, they might find something to give them an incentive to talk. They likely wanted to avoid having the police take a closer look at the books or deals made in that bar. She made a call but only reached a voicemail. She'd try again later.

Officer Sam Potts strode into the room purposefully, before halting in her tracks. She looked around. After some hesitation her gaze fell on Jordan.

"Oh, hey. Where is everybody?"

"Out, obviously. Can I help you?"

"Mr. Randall is here. He wants to speak to a detective. Do you know when Ellie will be back?"

"She's busy at the moment. I can talk to him."

"Really?" Sam blushed as if the possibility only now occurred to her.

Because she liked her, Jordan made an effort not to roll her eyes or show her frustration otherwise.

"Yes, really. Bring him in, please."

"Okay, then."

A few seconds later Jordan realized that Sam's hesitation was for a reason other than she doubted the capabilities of her pregnant colleague. Randall was wound tight.

"Is there anything new you can tell me?" he asked, foregoing any niceties. "It's been a few days, have you arrested the guy already?"

"The investigation is still ongoing," she said. "We are working with the local sheriff's office to resolve this as quickly as possible." Jordan had known that this wasn't the answer he wanted to hear.

"What more do you need? Elizabeth would have never gone with him freely!"

That was what they all thought, but they needed to prove it.

"We will figure out what happened," she said.

A door opened, and Ellie and Derek stepped out, not looking happy.

Behind them, Robert Hogan whispered with his defense lawyer, a smirk appearing on his face when he saw Matt Randall.

"Is that him? Is that the guy? You're letting him walk?"

In a move so quick it caught everyone off guard, he was at Hogan's throat, choking him.

Jordan half-heartedly got to her feet, though she knew there was no way she'd get in the middle of this—even when, not so long ago, she would have done so in a heartbeat.

"Mr. Randall, this is not helping!" Derek shouted. He restrained the distraught husband, while Ellie held back Hogan, his attorney looking on with interest.

"I don't give a shit! He murdered my wife, and you're letting him go!"

"I loved her," Hogan yelled back. "See? This is what she wanted to get away from!"

"Mr. Randall. Mr. Randall! Calm down."

Derek finally had some success after Ellie ushered Hogan and his lawyer outside.

"I guess that answers my question," Randall said sarcastically.

"This is serious," Derek told him. "Do not go near him."

"What's he going to do, sue me?"

Ellie returned, looking dejected. She had overheard Randall's words.

"He might, and he has witnesses, one of them his attorney. I understand where you're coming from, but this will only make him look sympathetic to a jury."

"Then you didn't do your fucking job."

He stormed out, and Jordan wondered if she owed Sam an apology coffee. And, what might have happened if Derek and Ellie hadn't been around. Her hand went to her belly before she became aware of it.

Ellie had a hard time concentrating when she met with the medical examiner, shaken by what she'd witnessed. She knew that Jordan would want to work until the last possible moment, and in general, she was okay with that. She had expressed sympathy when Jordan grumbled about tasks she considered rather mundane. The truth was Ellie was relieved to know that she'd be safe at the station, doing interviews, mostly by phone, and working on paperwork.

There had been an incident a few months ago where a suspect had attacked Ellie, but that happened in an interrogation room. Jamie Ryan had been tried and convicted. Matt Randall wasn't a suspect. Everyone could snap under pressure. Ellie forced her mind to leave worst case scenarios alone and focus on the work.

"Are you listening to me, or should I start from the beginning?" Ellie's state of mind hadn't gone unnoticed with Dr. Adams.

"I'm listening. Sorry."

"Obvious cause of death, the head wound."

"Yeah, I figured." Ellie reminded herself to take shallow breaths.

"Those stairs, they were concrete?"

"No, wood. There's a bit of a grass area and then concrete in the parking space."

"Take a look and tell me what you think," Dr. Adams prompted.

"Isn't that your job?" It didn't take Ellie long to realize what the ME meant, though. "It must have been a pretty hard fall. So, either it didn't happen on the stairs, or...she fell from higher up, or someone pushed her."

"Physics." Dr. Adams nodded.

"And any evidence we might've had was lost in the fire. Damn."

"I might have something else for you." She pointed out barely visible patches of discoloration around the woman's wrists. "A bit of residue of a sticky substance too, though it seems someone tried to wash it off."

"Duct tape!" Ellie said, having forgotten all about her earlier worries.

"We have yet to test for that, but I'm willing to guess, that's what it was."

"There's only so many ways he can spin this. We need to take a look at this guy's apartment."

"You might want to try and get a warrant after the tests come back," Dr. Adams advised.

"I don't know if we can wait that long. Evidence disappears around this guy."

"I'll see to it that someone gets back to you as soon as possible."

"Thank you."

"Don't worry. I appreciate the coffee, though," was Sam's answer. "You must be really excited now."

"I am," Jordan confessed. "In fact, I'm somewhere in between excited and wanting to take a nap most of the time. Oh, and off they go," she commented on Derek and Ellie leaving for Hogan's apartment.

"You wish you could go?" At least, Sam was finally losing her reservations.

"Actually? No. I think we had enough excitement for the day. I'm just glad this is moving forward."

Back at her desk, Jordan tried the number again, and this time, her call was answered.

"Jordan Carpenter," Veronica Sawyer said as if unsure who the person calling her was.

"A friend of Taylor's," Jordan supplied.

On the other end, Veronica started laughing. "Come on, it hasn't been that long! Of course I remember you. You're still in Homicide?"

"Yes."

"How's Bethany?"

"Good, I suppose."

"Oh, I sense a longer story. What do you need? And don't try to tell me otherwise. You guys always need something."

Veronica wasn't so wrong. Jordan could remember a few cases when her insights had helped their work, though she hadn't seen much of her after she'd met Bethany. She assumed that Taylor Hudson, Jordan's friend and colleague at the time, had kept in touch.

The club Veronica, her husband and friends belonged to was the complete opposite of what Jordan had witnessed up in the cabin. They were proud of their very different reputation, though they might be aware of bad behavior close to home.

She described the bar where she and Derek had gone to make the phone call. When she had finished, Veronica responded with a frustrated sound.

"Damn, yes, I've heard of the place. Looks like it's falling apart, but it hasn't been around all that long. I hear they are connected to some unpleasant folks."

"How unpleasant?"

"Oh, you know. Not Homicide unpleasant, not yet anyway, but pretty much everything else. I bet everyone you saw in there was white too."

Jordan remembered the looks and the muttered comments too, vividly so.

"Problem is, we have a very suspicious-looking accident that happened close by, and someone might have witnessed something. They're not likely to talk to us unless…"

"Unless they see a reason. All right. I can ask some of the guys. I'll get back to you."

"Can we meet? You could come by after my shift."

"I suppose your address changed too?"

"It has. I'll text you. See you later."

"Whatever you're looking for, you're not going to find it here," Hogan had predicted with a smile, and unfortunately, he'd been right. His apartment was tidy, though it didn't look like it had been staged for them. Something was bothering Ellie though.

"You said that you and Elizabeth were in a long-term relationship, but you have no pictures of her, anywhere."

He shrugged. "I wouldn't have left them up while my tenant was here. Besides, she didn't like me to take pictures. I didn't know why at the time, but of course, with the husband having a temper like this, I can't say I blame her for being paranoid. Do you?"

Ellie left his question unanswered.

"There were some red marks on her wrists. Do you have any explanation for that?"

"Red marks?" Hogan looked puzzled. "Must have been those bracelets she was wearing. Cheap stuff, but she liked them for a reason, so I didn't say anything."

"We also found some sticky residue on her skin. Please, think carefully. Is there anything else you want to tell us?"

"I think I know where you're going with this, and I don't like it. Betty and I might not have been in a traditional relationship, but I can assure you, it was true love. I hope you'll never have to go through what I am going through now. It was a tragic accident. If only Betty was here to tell you herself."

"So, you no longer think that one of the patrons at the bar had something to do with her death?"

"What? I never said that. She fell. I found her. I told you and the sheriff many times."

They weren't going to learn anything here.

"Oh my God, what happened to you?" Despite her dramatic entrance, Veronica was quite happy for her, hugging Jordan closely. "You know I hate those clichés, but you are actually glowing. What else did you keep from me? There's no guy living here, is there?"

It only took one look to disavow her of that notion.

"Forget I asked. There's another lady living here."

"Ellie," Jordan said. "We're married. She's a cop too." This summed up her life in pretty amazing ways, though she hadn't invited Veronica to catch up. Maybe another time. There was too much on her mind to go there now.

"Wow. A lot of things have changed since I last saw you."

A lot of things Jordan didn't want to rehash.

"You've seen Taylor lately?" She had to ask though.

"Not in a long time. Greg and I bought a house though." That was almost enough to distract Jordan. "Well, we all need time to relax and breathe sometimes," Veronica said with a shrug. "So—about those guys up in the mountains. I asked around, and as you can imagine, none of us are friendly with them. There have been some clashes with the owners of other cabins and resorts in the area because of political meetings."

"Of what kind?"

"The far-right BS kind—and not just guys on bikes. Suits, too. Apparently, the owner turns a blind eye."

"Classy." Jordan didn't even try to suppress the shudder. "We'll definitely have to take a closer look. This case is too bizarre already. It wouldn't surprise me if they were involved somehow."

"I imagine you're not the one going to take that closer look," Veronica said as if Jordan needed a reminder.

"I'm not sure what this is about exactly, but I think I agree." Ellie, who had just come in, stopped at the sight of Veronica. "Hi."

"Hi. You must be Ellie." Veronica got up to shake Ellie's hand. "I'll admit I haven't heard much yet, because most personal things are on a need-to-know basis with Carpenter, but you got her pregnant, so that's serious. I'm Veronica."

"Nice to meet you," Ellie said, looking intrigued. She seemed equally amused and startled by the joke.

"Veronica once was an informant for a friend of mine," Jordan supplied. "She has some interesting insights about the folks up at the bar."

"Okay...That's good. I'm pretty much out of insights, and Hogan isn't budging. He seems to have an explanation for everything. It's all a bit far-fetched, but in the end, it will mean reasonable doubt." She looked from Jordan to Veronica who had taken a seat again, crossing her long legs. Jordan could basically see the question forming on Ellie's mind, and she'd have to make sure there were no misunderstandings. Veronica was married to her bike first, and her husband of over fifteen years, Greg, second. She had been a good friend to Taylor though, who had been someone in Jordan's life before she met Bethany. So long ago it almost wasn't true. It certainly didn't matter anymore.

"We can talk about all of this over dinner?" she offered.

"Sure," Ellie agreed. "You'd like to stay?"

"If that's okay with you?" Veronica looked a little too intrigued for Jordan's comfort, but she couldn't say no to her now. So far, Ellie had taken all trips down Jordan's memory lanes in stride—this one would be no exception. Hopefully.

After ordering in Chinese food, Ellie set the table for three.

"Would you like a beer, or a glass of wine?" she asked their guest.

"No thanks," Veronica said. "Water is fine. So...You're a Homicide detective too?"

"I am."

"How long have you two been working together?"

"A few years," Jordan answered for her. "And right now, we could really use something to move this case forward."

Veronica cast her an amused smile, but she took the hint.

"Just as well we discuss this before food because it's pretty bad. A friend of mine once dated a guy who got entangled with them. We got her out."

"What's their deal?" Ellie asked, once more petrified at the thought of what might have happened the night Jordan and Derek went to the bar.

Veronica shrugged. "The guys there think of themselves as super manly, but in fact they're just the hired hands of some extreme right organization. The guys at the top won't get their hands dirty, but they need someone to help rile up their audience. If your guy had contacts there, he might have been one of the people telling them what to do."

That was a new avenue. So far, the connection of Hogan and the bikers had seemed more like an accidental one.

"I hope we'll get one of them to talk," Ellie said. "I want us to unravel this some more, learn more about Elizabeth Randall's last moments. Anything that will help us hold him accountable." She caught Jordan's serious gaze, fairly sure she knew what was on her mind. They had met their share of Hogans on the job.

"I hope this helps you," Veronica said.

"We'll put the pieces together eventually. We don't quite have the link between him being a part of that group, and a psychopath stalker, but perhaps one of his buddies can help."

"They might if you lean on them hard enough. They don't want the FBI to come looking."

"I'll talk to Derek, and we'll go back there tomorrow," Ellie said to Jordan. "And here's the food," she added as the doorbell rang. "Just in time."

Veronica stayed for coffee and a piece of cheesecake. Soon after she left, Ellie and Jordan settled in for the night, though Ellie wasn't ready to go to sleep yet after everything she'd learned.

"So...about that part of your life you've kept secret. When you used to hang out with biker chicks."

"That is not an apt description of the situation," Jordan said, though she sounded amused. "Good night. I love you."

"Come on. You can't sleep anyway."

"That's true." With a sigh, Jordan turned to her. "Although, there's nothing much to tell you haven't already heard. She helped me and Taylor out on some cases."

"Taylor Hudson, your friend."

"That's right. Look, there's no story. We went on a few dates. I guess you could say I never looked outside of work. It doesn't matter though. I'm happy where I am now."

"Yes, me too." Even after everything they'd shared and went through, Ellie found it amazing to realize those differences between them. "I never really dated anyone at work before. You were my first, and you're going to be my only one."

Jordan laughed softly. "It was always amazing to me how anyone managed to meet someone not in law enforcement."

"I did some traveling," Ellie said. "After my parents died...It threw me off completely. I took a year off from school, worked here and there. For a while, I just floated."

"I'm really sorry."

"Don't be. It wasn't all bad." Ellie remembered and cherished the good sides, conversations and insights, the encounters that made her return with renewed determination and clarity—facing her pain and her dreams alike. "I would love to show you some of those places. Maybe someday when Meri is old enough, we just go on the road for a few weeks."

"Yes, maybe we will."

The idea struck them both as funny, because based on the past few years it would be tough to find the time for that.

Chapter Six

After sorting out the information Veronica Sawyer had given them, Ellie and Derek returned to the bar the following afternoon. Ellie was lost in thought, happy to let Derek drive. She barely refrained from asking him if he'd ever met Taylor Hudson. A few years ago, she might have been a tad insecure. These days, she was simply curious.

They stopped for a quick coffee before turning onto the road that led them to the bar. There were only a few motorcycles parked outside.

"Quite the difference from a weekend," Derek remarked.

Confronted with the sight of the run-down bar, Ellie couldn't hold a comment of her own. "You've got to be kidding me."

"Well, it was my understanding that you wanted me to keep an eye on her. Don't tell her I said that. We were just trying to get to the damn phone," he said dryly. "But wait 'til you get inside."

"Oh boy."

"Yeah."

Ellie hesitated for a moment. "Look, I know it might come across as bitchy, but between this place, and the fistfight breaking out at the station, I'm kind of freaking out. I know Jordan has been doing the job since before I came along, but we've never had a baby before."

"I'm sure she understands." He chuckled. "I do too. I'm kind of used to her telling me things she doesn't want you to know in order to protect you."

"Yes, I imagine that's happened a time or two. Okay, let's do this? There's still a chance we'll get dinner at a decent time."

"Sounds good to me."

The man behind the bar wiping the counter recognized Derek. "You again. Ditched the pregnant chick?"

Derek cleared his throat which was, Ellie assumed, mostly for her.

"Detective Harding," she said. "You met Detective Henderson. You know this guy?" she asked, showing him a photograph of Robert Hogan on her phone.

"Hm, I don't know. He doesn't look like he's a regular here."

"Try. Maybe he just came by a time or two."

She became aware of the bartender's gaze going to a place somewhere past her shoulder, and Derek turning as well. On the other end of the bar, two men were watching them cautiously, one of them moving towards the door. Ellie turned to walk towards them.

"Hi, I'm Detective Harding. I'd like to ask—" Even as she spoke those words, she knew he was going to run. The story of her life.

Fortunately, the man gave up after stumbling over tree roots only about ten feet away from the cabin. He scrambled to his feet, eyes darting around as if looking for an escape.

"Relax, man. We just have a few questions."

"I don't need to answer your questions," he seethed.

"A woman died not far from here, and we're trying to figure out what happened—or who might have seen anything."

"What does that have to do with me?"

Ellie barely kept herself from rolling her eyes. "Probably nothing, but why did you run?"

"Sheriff is looking to plant something on us. Why would you be any different?"

"Because we want to know what happened to her. That's the most important thing here, not the couple of grams in your pocket. Do you know him?"

His eyes widened just a bit. Ellie hadn't missed it.

"That's the guy whose cabin went up in flames. I saw him on the news."

"Okay. Did you ever see him before?"

"No. Never."

"Are you sure?" Derek, who had followed them, pressed.

The man didn't answer, but he was all but squirming.

"Anyone else ever mention him?" Ellie added.

A shrug was all she got. Ellie didn't believe for a second that he was telling the truth, so she shifted gears.

"Look, this is our priority right now. Top of the list. But we've been told that there are the occasional political meetings at your favorite hangout, something people above our pay grade might be interested in. If you have nothing more to tell us, perhaps we could send them to take a look."

"We don't mess around with those guys," he said nervously.

"Why don't we go back inside, and you tell us a bit more?" she asked.

Jordan checked her watch and cast a glance at her meticulous desk. Derek and Ellie had not yet returned. She was likely going to have dinner by herself tonight. They were overdue for some grocery shopping, she thought guiltily. She did have more time than Ellie, but trips to the grocery store were exhausting and frustrating these days. Every once in a while, she thought about Kathryn, going through the same thing as a teenager, with no one to help her or listen. Given the time and her age, Jordan could only imagine the stares and whispers.

Dr. Burns, Ellie, and everyone else who had supported Jordan, had been right—her side of the story didn't change. Her experiences and emotions, as a child, and now, were still valid. She had a more complete picture now.

"Hey. I was hoping I'd find you here. Do you have a moment?"

She looked up, fairly surprised to see Major Crimes Detective Noah Shriver. They had worked on a couple of cases some months ago, and he had indicated he was interested in a position in Homicide. So far, it hadn't happened, though he'd tried hard to make connections.

"Sure. You'd like a coffee? I'm not going to have one, obviously."

He looked around, his gaze falling on Maria Doss working on her desk.

"I was hoping for somewhere more private."

What could they have to discuss that was so private the break room wouldn't do?

"Please," he said.

"I could go for dinner, if you'd like to join me," she offered after a moment of consideration. "Just give me a second."

"Sure. Thank you."

Ellie and Derek wouldn't be done for a while to come, but perhaps they'd join them later.

※

The man finally sat down with them in a corner of the bar, keeping an eye on the exit and the bartender alternately.

"I don't know anything about those meetings. I just come here to have a few beers, that's all."

"What about him?" Ellie prompted as she put her phone on the table.

"He's been around, barely talks to anyone. I've seen him at the hardware store, buying stuff for the cabin, I suppose."

It was a long shot, but she had to cross a few items off her list. "You remember when?"

"Not that long ago, a couple of weeks? I hear he lived there, maybe just getting ready for the winter."

"And when he came to the bar, who did he talk to?"

He shrugged. "Mostly Brad."

"The bartender?"

"Yep, that's him. Like I told you, he wasn't really the type to talk much to anyone. And no, I don't know what they talked about, but Brad has his own cabin out there. That's all I know. I swear."

Ellie had the feeling this conversation was steadily going nowhere, and she could tell from Derek's gaze that he thought the same. They were no closer to proving Hogan had lied to them.

"Hey. You'd like some of that cheesecake Pauline says I need to keep in the fridge?" Jack asked before giving her a hug.

"No thanks," Jordan declined with a laugh. "We came here for dinner."

"Mr. Carpenter."

Shriver had been to the *SEVEN* before, the bar that Jack had built back up from the ground with friends of his. He had been trying hard to make friends, but Jordan hadn't seen him here in a long time. She had chosen the place because it was familiar and close by. Perhaps there was another reason as well, but she wasn't sure yet.

"What can I get you?" Jack asked, curiosity in his gaze.

"Ellie will be here later, but I couldn't wait," she said lightly, answering his unspoken question. I'll have a club sandwich with fries and an ice tea...you?"

"I'll start with a beer," Shriver answered. "No, wait, give me a vodka too."

Jack cast a look at Jordan who shrugged. She was intrigued, but clueless.

"All right. Coming right up."

They chose a table in a corner, the silence starting to turn awkward soon.

"So, what's this all about?"

"I took your advice," he said. "Made connections, checked in with Lieutenant Carroll. Worked my ass off meanwhile. Nothing."

"I'm sorry. That's frustrating."

"That's not how it usually works, I've been told." Their drinks arrived, and he downed the vodka shot in one. "What the hell—get me another one?" he asked the waiter.

"Slow down. I was under the impression you wanted to talk? What's this really about?"

She could see that Jack was still behind the counter, keeping an eye on them. Jordan appreciated the general idea, though she didn't think there was any danger coming from a colleague frustrated with a current lack of prospects. And even if there was, she could still take care of herself, damn it.

"I think you're aware that people talk a lot about your unit. What happened with Waters, and your wife being promoted to detective very quickly."

"Wait. What people? And I can't believe you're falling for this crap."

"There's nothing to it then?"

"Ellie went through all the hoops she had to go through, that had nothing to do with Waters' decision to retire, or the fact that he blew his pension, because he thought it was a good idea to assault an officer." The words came out fairly calmly, which spoke of her self-control. "You want friends in Homicide, you better tell me who's spreading gossip."

His second vodka arrived, but Shriver picked up his beer bottle instead.

"You must admit it's curious. Another officer was suspended earlier this year. Harding's name came up again."

"Sure it did, because when she requested back-up, he turned off the scanner and turned the other way. There was an investigation, and he came back. Certainly, this is not behavior Lieutenant Daniels, or any other boss would like to see?"

"Yeah, I know what you mean," he said, picking up the other shot and setting it down again. "That wasn't okay."

"So, we've cleared this?" Jordan wasn't sure if she believed him. It seemed too quick and easy. He had given the gossip around their unit this much consideration. That made her wonder if he was someone she'd want to work with on a daily basis. Ellie had worked hard to get where she was, and the position hadn't fallen into her lap. "Who did you talk to?"

"Different people at the precinct. They say it's no secret she wanted the job, and she got it, and they're wondering how it happened so fast. I thought you should know it's not just about Waters."

Jordan almost wanted that shot. She and Ellie had enough to think about without the rumor mill acting up again.

"Well, thanks, but if you want advice, pay no attention to any of it. It's not true, period. Ellie made it to where she is because she works damn hard, and she's good at her job. That's all."

"They're talking about you too."

"I can imagine. I'm pretty hard to overlook these days." It bothered her that she still hadn't figured out what his deal was. Shriver had shown focus when they worked together. Now, he just seemed off.

"No, not that. The serial killer case. I didn't realize that was you."

"Well, now you know." Jordan forced a smile and got up. "I'm going to check on that sandwich. Be right back."

When she passed by the bar, Jack commented, "Everything okay? That guy is wound tight."

So, it wasn't just her and hormones making her paranoid. Jordan hadn't thought so. "He sure is. It's okay. I just need the restroom for a moment. Keep my plate warm for me?"

"Of course."

Inside the restroom, she took a moment to get her bearings, frustrated that people she'd rely on in a sticky situation had nothing better to do than to speculate about her and Ellie's life. Could it be that Shriver had misunderstood something? Why would he lie to her? He was obviously upset with something, but was the stalling of his career aspirations enough of an explanation? Or was there an underlying issue? Come to think of it, she didn't know him all that well. He'd been to their house once. She'd had a couple of interactions with his boss, Lieutenant Daniels, and found her to be fair. She wasn't sure why he was in such a hurry.

When she left the restroom, Jordan was relieved to find that Ellie and Derek had arrived. Shriver wouldn't go back to any of the previous subjects with the two of them around.

"I'll be right with you," Jordan said and went back to the table where Shriver had somehow managed to get another shot and call himself a cab. The beer bottle was empty.

"You'll be okay to get home?"

His gaze was slightly unfocused, but he nodded.

"Forget all the noise, okay? You did everything you could, and I'm sure Carroll will let you know if there's an opening. Have a good night."

It was all she could do for him. Jordan still felt a tad spooked that he'd brought up *that* case out of the blue, but it had made national headlines. It wasn't that much of a surprise that people were still talking about it. She just didn't want to. Ever.

Finally, she got to enjoy her dinner in the company of her wife and friends.

"So," Derek remarked, "what part of 'you're going to have a baby with this lady' doesn't he understand?"

There it was. Her previous work with Shriver had caused a bit of tension and misunderstandings, though reflecting on the recent conversation, Jordan couldn't blame him.

"He's been bothering you?" Ellie asked.

"No. You're all wrong. He's just pissed he hasn't been able to get into Homicide yet, and he's been listening to all the wrong people."

I didn't realize that was you.

That guy is wound tight.

It certainly wasn't her business, but she felt uneasy, like there was something she had overlooked.

"Let's forget about him. How did it go with your guy earlier?"

Ellie sighed. "I'm sure he knows something, but he told us just enough so we can't bust him yet. I'd like a trace on him and Hogan. I'll talk it through with Valerie tomorrow."

"We get to go back again and talk to Brad the bartender. Fun times." Derek made a non-committal sound. "All that gas should count for expenses."

"I want to talk to the sheriff as well," Ellie said. "See where they are on the arson. I swear he's avoiding me on the phone."

Jordan listened to their conversation with an emotion she couldn't quite pinpoint. Perhaps at this moment, she understood Shriver a bit more than she'd been willing to admit—with the exception that she knew for sure she'd be back.

"What about the political angle?" she asked.

"That was mostly to get him to talk, but it might be worth it to get in touch with the FBI as well."

"I can give Nina a call."

"That would be great." Ellie gave her a grateful smile as she stole one of the fries off Jordan's plate. "Thank you."

Carroll hadn't chosen her because of favoritism or because of her connection to Jordan. Budget concerns were always an issue, but perhaps Waters' story had convinced the lieutenant that their group, for now, worked best the way it was. Jordan couldn't agree more.

⸺◈⸺

Why didn't she believe him? She had to understand that he had only her best interests at heart—his, too, of course, but the two went together. The people around her only enabled her. They had no intention of helping her on the right path. He would when the time was right, and she'd be so grateful to him. He knew it.

He just had to be more patient, revise and adjust the plan.

Nothing much made him feel good these days, but the plan always did.

It would come to pass eventually.

Chapter Seven

E llie had gotten out of bed early to get ready for work and prepare breakfast. When she went to the bathroom, Jordan was still sleeping. A few minutes later, as Ellie started a pot of decaf in the kitchen, Jordan emerged from the guest bathroom, looking pale and tired.

"Hey. Everything okay?"

"Yeah. Remind me to take a break on the fried food for a while."

"You'd prefer a tea?" Ellie brushed her hand over Jordan's back, rubbing gently before she went to pour herself some coffee.

"No, thanks. This is fine. I think."

"You could take the morning. Or even the day. You certainly have enough hours. Though I'd almost prefer it if you were at work so I can keep an eye on you."

Jordan's smile seemed forced.

"I'm serious."

"No, I'm okay. I might take an hour or so, but I'll call Nina as soon as I come in." Nina Torres had worked with them on several cases as a liaison with the FBI.

"Take your time. Do you want me to stay here with you? I'll just let Derek know, and we'll go together when you're ready."

"No, you have things to do. I'll be fine. I'll let you know what Nina said. Go," she added with a bit more determination. "*We*'ll be fine."

To Ellie's relief, she sounded a lot more convincing than a few minutes ago. As much as she would have liked to spend the morning at home with Jordan, Ellie had a list of people to see: A.D.A. Esposito, Sheriff Watkins, and the bartender. Perhaps she could be lucky and find Brad Sellers at home before he opened the bar.

"Okay. I'll see you later."

Being pregnant, for the most part, had surprised her. The morning sickness had been taxing. For someone who had never had to give much thought about finding clothes that fit, her changing shape represented a challenge—until Ellie insisted that they go see Rhonda Marks, Ellie's ex who worked in a charming boutique that had a surprising choice of maternity clothes. It might have been awkward, but Ellie had been so happy and proud it was clear she wasn't trying to get even for all the times Jordan's exes had been in their lives, professionally.

The greatest surprise for Jordan was that all those lingering fears she'd had up until the pregnancy test and confirmation by her doctor, had been dissipating over time. She knew she and Ellie would do the best possible for this child, and that they had many opportunities to do so. She believed that they would do well.

Nevertheless, as Jordan finally locked the door behind herself to drive to work, she had to admit she felt antsy. Nothing surprising about that, really. She was ready, or at least she thought she was. The date wasn't coming fast enough, and still, it would be too soon.

The trip to the cabin should have been a relaxing event before starting to slow down, but the past few days hadn't been relaxing or slow. She wasn't sure if it was the image of Robert Hogan's bloody hands that haunted her or Shriver's near debilitating doubts. One claimed he had lost the love of his life, the other thought he was being denied the career he deserved.

Even Meri seemed antsy, but maybe she was just as eager to be in the world as Jordan wanted her to be. And then what? How to make sure she'd never run into men who thought of women as possessions—or the women who indulged them? Was Hogan one of those men? He might have been stalking Elizabeth Randall for years.

What about the biker bar and its patrons' connections to sinister ideologies? She thought of Ariel whom they had rescued from a women-hating cult. The worst-case scenarios were often closer than the general public thought.

She parked her car and took the elevator up to her floor. On ground level, A.D.A. Valerie Esposito got on.

"Good morning, Detective," she remarked. "Good timing too. I believe everyone is waiting for us."

They met in the briefing room where Derek, Ellie and the lieutenant were already present. Maria Doss came in, coffee in hand, exchanging a quick smile with Valerie, and everyone took their seats.

"All right, let's get started," Carroll said. "Harding."

For all her dire thoughts this morning, Jordan barely suppressed a smile when Ellie started to lay out their findings and strategy. She was in awe. She remembered the admiring looks, at the old *Code Seven* and at roll call, Ellie's determination and embrace of her dreams that made her impossible to resist. Ellie still looked at her like that, and at the same time, she was aware of her own skills and potential, had used it to her advantage. Everyone could see that she belonged here.

"...and notify Agent Torres. You'll get back to me on that?"

It took Jordan a second or so to realize Ellie had addressed her, and she nodded. "Sure."

Valerie snickered, and Ellie continued.

"So, we'll have to wait for the warrant to come through, but there's nothing that says we can't start with the sheriff and talk to the bartender as well. He lives in town. The lab should get back to me sometime soon, today hopefully."

"I'll get the ball rolling on the warrant," Valerie said.

"About those expenses..." Derek started, earning a groan from the lieutenant.

"Write it up, Henderson, I'll see what I can do."

"No one else is complaining, and they have a baby on the way," Maria remarked, shaking her head.

"Well, I have a Goddaughter and a boat on the way," Derek countered good-naturedly.

"That's enough. All of you, out of here now."

Everyone followed the lieutenant's command. Jordan found the familiar banter a relief, though a hint of wariness remained. It was probably just her body telling her that those fries had been a bad idea. She went to get herself a tea from the vending machine before she called Nina Torres.

◦⌐◦

Ellie was driving while Derek stared out of the window morosely.

"Well, look on the bright side," she offered. "The sights are breathtaking."

"I wasn't kidding though. It's starting to get expensive that we have to keep coming out here. Honestly, I'm surprised that Uncle Jackson wanted to buy in this area. Lots of unfriendly people around."

Ellie was beginning to understand that there was more that bothered Derek about this town than the gas price. Given her own experiences with residents and the sheriff's office even, she could sympathize.

"At some point, we're going to wrap up here. Perhaps even get that bar closed. Everything in there screams health and fire hazard."

"Closing down a bar won't get crazy ideas out of people's heads." Unfortunately, he had a point.

"You're right. Let's just get this done, okay?"

<hr />

"Hey, good to hear from you. How's everything over there?" Nina Torres sounded surprisingly cheerful.

"Pretty good actually, thanks. I could use your help on something."

"I assumed. What can I do for you?"

Jordan related the recent case and the spotty information they had about far-right political meetings connected to the biker bar and its bartender, Brad Sellers.

"This is all on the periphery so far," she explained. "We have a suspicious accident that looks too damn much like a homicide, but if there's anything else going on, you might know about it?"

"Chances are the local press and a lot of people in town know about it too," Nina mused. "These people are pretty brazen these days. Do you have any idea if someone had a hand in your homicide?"

"So far, potential witnesses who might or might not have a reason to turn on our suspect."

"That's all you have?"

"I know it's not much."

"No, it's not, but I'll see what I can do."

"Thanks. I appreciate it."

"Always. Oh, hang on a second."

Jordan took a sip of her sufficiently cooled down tea while waiting for her to return.

"Hi, Jordan. How are you doing?"

The person on the other end was not Nina Torres, and not someone she had expected to talk to today.

"Bethany. Hi. I'm good. You?"

"Well, if you follow the news, that's a pretty good barometer of how I am these days." Bethany sighed. "People used to think we were the good guys, now it's a new conspiracy theory every other day. At times I wonder if I should have become the lawyer my parents wanted me to be—it seems like there'd be more money in it. Anyway. Nina tells me you have some questions about Sellers and his charming little place. I could send you some reading material of an investigation we did a few years ago."

"Not sure if it's the same people we're interested in but thank you."

After a few seconds of silence, Bethany asked, "So, what else is new with you?"

Jordan looked down at her belly, wondering if she wanted to have that conversation now, or ever. She decided against it.

"Nothing much. Work."

Sorry, Meri.

"Well, I'll leave you to it, then," Bethany said. "I'll send you those files later. Have a good day."

"You too. Thank you."

Those next few weeks were supposed to be smooth sailing. Smooth sailing and addressing what was the most important development in her life at the moment, did not go together.

Sheriff Watkins didn't have much news for them. They hadn't found the arsonist, and regarding Sellers and the bar, there had been a few noise complaints over the years—none for alleged political meetings.

Ellie could sense that Derek barely refrained from rolling his eyes or react in a similar manner.

"Yeah, I think we're done here," he said. "Thanks so much for your cooperation."

Watkins didn't seem to notice or mind the sarcasm.

They hadn't heard from the lab or Valerie, so they decided to stop for lunch in town before heading to see Sellers.

Food would lift Derek's spirits, Ellie reasoned, and she desperately needed some caffeine.

Next, as planned, they went to Brad Sellers' house. Ellie had to knock three times before he opened the door looking like he had just gotten out of bed, blinking against the sunlight.

"This is getting annoying," he complained.

"Well, too bad for you. It's murder that annoys us. And lies."

"I didn't lie about anything."

"Robert Hogan frequented your bar."

He gave Derek a stubborn stare. "Frequent is a fancy word to say he's been in there a time or two."

"We heard that you're the only one he talked to," Ellie supplied.

Sellers shrugged. "Yeah, well, I poured him the drinks. Pour fellow was a little out of place if you know what I mean."

"What did he talk about?"

"This and that."

"A little more precise, please."

"Just stuff. About his tenant, and his girlfriend. Seemed like one or the other bothered him at different times. But if you want to know if he confessed to killing anyone, no, not to me. He came in, had a few drinks, left."

"Did you ever see him with the girlfriend?" Ellie asked, remembering Hogan claiming the bikers had given them the "evil eye."

"No, never saw her. Is that all?"

Unfortunately, that was all. Ellie wondered how far Jordan had gotten.

⁂

So far, Jordan had not found anything useful in the files Bethany had sent her, though they made for an interesting and disturbing read. Even before Sellers, the former owner had hosted a couple of far-right groups that were trying to set foot in the door of mainstream politics. At the time of the investigation, there had been a few complaints about attempts to intimidate other business owners and residents, and the suspects in question had enough connections to get the FBI involved. In the end, most of the accusations were withdrawn, only a small number of individuals convicted.

She kept reading up until the name Sellers came up. While the establishment had always been considered a local biker hangout in the first place, the political players and wannabes were from out of town.

And then there was an interview with a Robert Hogan who admitted he'd had some dealings with one of the persons of interest but claimed he didn't know about their political leanings.

The transcript of a wire tap that showed Hogan taking part in a lively discussion about how the infiltration of local governments was necessary and the best first step to reach their goals.

Every time they uncovered a new layer to this man, the picture became more unpleasant.

Ellie's phone rang. Getting to her feet and over to her desk as quickly as possible, Jordan picked it up. The lab tech confirmed that the traces of sticky substance on Elizabeth Randall's wrists were consistent with duct tape, and that someone had tried to remove them with an alcohol-like substance.

Jordan hoped that Ellie and Derek were within cell phone range again.

As she picked up her own phone, she saw someone familiar exit Lieutenant Carroll's office—Lieutenant Daniels of Major Crimes, Detective Noah Shriver's boss. Jordan wondered how aware she was of Shriver's complaints.

Daniels stopped by her desk on the way out.

"Detective Carpenter, hello."

"Lieutenant." The woman's terse expression made Jordan curious as to what she'd discussed with Carroll.

"I see there have been some exciting developments since we last met," she said, now with a smile. "Seven months?"

"Almost eight now."

"Oh, I remember that."

"Don't tell me. It gets worse before it gets better?"

"It does, but I promise you it's worth it. Until they're teenagers that is, then you'll wonder why all over again."

"Well, we have a lot of time until then."

"True. I'll let you get back to work now. See you next time."

She hesitated a brief moment, and Jordan almost expected her to address something else. Daniels turned to walk away.

Jordan tried Ellie's cell phone, to no avail.

Chapter Eight

Ellie had suggested going back to the bar. They couldn't search the inside, yet, but something told her that they could find more answers there.

"I swear, last stop and then we go home."

"If you say so."

"Think of the boat you're going to buy soon."

"I don't know. The lieutenant didn't seem convinced when he said to write up those expenses."

"I'm sure it will be okay. Let's get this over with?"

They got out of the car in the parking space, a couple of motorcycles standing next to the concrete wall that framed the parking.

"What are you trying to find here? No one's talking anyway. Unless we find proof that some of them are planning a coup against the government, there's not much we can do."

"Yeah, I know. I just want to take a quick look, and then we can head back. Oh see..." she said, holding up her cell phone. "Jordan found something, and the lab came back, and..." She showed him the message. "The warrant came through. We can go in after all."

"Hallelujah," Derek exclaimed. "This might actually be the last time we come here."

"You're never going to invite us to the cabin again?"

"We'll see. For now, I really need a break from this town."

They got out of the car and walked towards the bar when they heard a sound from inside.

"I wonder who's there. The place is closed, and Sellers didn't have enough time to make it here before us," Ellie remarked.

They cautiously inched closer to the window. Ellie couldn't see anyone, so she assumed the noise must have come from the backroom where the office was located. The door to the main room was open, and they went inside, barely a couple of steps into the bar when the shot rang out.

"You've got to be kidding me," Derek muttered as they both ran for the office door.

Slumped over the desk was Robert Hogan, bleeding heavily from a gunshot wound in his back. The window was open, a cold draft coming in.

"Stay with him," Derek said. Outside, the person fleeing was revving up the engine of one of the motorcycles. Derek ran back outside.

Ellie looked around to find something to put pressure on the wound. Her only choice was a dishtowel that didn't look all that clean. She cursed as her cell phone showed no service once again and used the landline to call 911.

❦

Robert Hogan wasn't dead, but he was barely hanging in there. Derek had stayed behind to search the bar, while Ellie followed the ambulance and then the gurney into the hospital.

Hogan was fading in and out.

"Mr. Hogan, it's Detective Harding. Can you tell us who shot you?" She was so focused on him that she almost ran into the doctor who blocked her in front of the double door to the E.R.

"Detective! You can't go in there."

"He's awake! Perhaps he can answer—"

"Not now." His tone was final. "We'll notify you."

Ellie had no choice but to step back. She went back outside to call Derek, hoping she could reach his cell. Her mind was racing with questions. Who had Hogan met in the bar? And was there someone who wanted him dead—other than Matt Randall? To her relief, Derek answered.

"Hey. Did you find anything?"

"A bunch of documents that might be interesting," he answered. "I'm on my way back to the station. Meet you there?"

"They didn't let me speak to Hogan, and they don't know if he's going to make it. I'll wait."

"All right, I'll take this back and go over it with Jordan."

"What about Randall?" Ellie asked. Given the nature of the situation, and what happened last time he'd come to the department, she didn't want Jordan anywhere near him.

"I'll have Maria pick him up. I'll see you later?"

"Sure. Thanks."

Ellie suppressed a sigh. There was no saying how long this would take.

A new picture was unfolding about Hogan. The more layers they uncovered, the more unpleasant it got—it seemed that not only was he a stalker, but he had been contributing to far-right and white supremacist groups. It should have turned her stomach, but Jordan was hungry and jonesing for the cheesecake she had turned down the other day. Instead, she stuck with tea. Derek, who had arrived with boxes of papers they needed to go through, had brought a coffee for himself, and they worked quietly.

"Detective Carpenter?"

"Yes?" She looked up, blinking at the delivery man who was carrying a considerably sized gift basket, filled with chocolates. "Wow. Yes. That's me," she said. Derek whistled, and Jordan decided not to deign it with a reaction.

"Sign here, please? Enjoy."

"Thank you."

She found the small card attached, with a short note. *Hope you'll accept this as my apology. N.S.*

"You got a secret admirer?" Derek asked, amused, when they were alone again. Maria Doss had taken Randall to an interview room. On the other side of the room, a uniformed officer was giving the basket a longing look. "Or...not so secret?"

"Oh, shut up," Jordan muttered. She would have preferred if Shriver just wanted to forget about that strange episode. That would make it less awkward in case his aspirations ever came true. More and more, she was wondering what the atmosphere over at Major Crimes was like.

"You're worried about this guy?"

Derek's tone had changed, and obviously he had figured out who sent the basket.

Should she be? Jordan shook her head. Waters and Atwood were the exceptions. Shriver was dealing with some issues at the moment, but this was simply a polite gesture.

"No, not really. But I'll tell you something, get me another tea and I'll share what's in there."

"What did he say?"

"Forget about it. It's just an apology."

"For what?"

"Getting drunk in my face and repeating all the old rumors that have been floating around. It's nothing, really. But I could use a break, and this tea is cold."

"I'm on it," Derek said, getting up, though he didn't sound convinced.

Jordan picked up a pair of scissors from her desk and started to cut away the cellophane, thinking that in all her years on the job, she hadn't had a male colleague send her a gift like this. Odd indeed, but perhaps now they could forget about everything. That, and she appreciated the sweet treat. It didn't look like Ellie would be able to get here anytime soon.

A resident found Ellie to tell her that Hogan was still in surgery. They'd call her as soon as, or—if—she'd be able to talk to him. The surgeon, who had brushed her off earlier hadn't come out to inform her. This told her that the situation was serious. Hogan might not wake up, but if he did, she'd have to come back the next day. She knew Derek had caught a ride back with one of the uniforms, but she drove by the bar anyway. One of the motorcycles was still in the parking lot. The bar was closed, of course, crime scene tape indicating the incident that happened here earlier. Even with the spotty cell phone reception in this area, she had understood that Jordan found something about Hogan's relations to far-right political groups. There was probably more in the papers that Derek had brought to the station. Would those give them a hint as to who had attempted to kill Hogan?

She flashed back on her and Derek following the biker who had told them Hogan used to talk to Sellers only.

What did she hope to find that wasn't in the papers? Ellie wasn't sure. The daylight was fading, and she still had a considerable drive in front of her. Still, she walked around the bar, uncertain what she was hoping to find. She climbed on top of the small concrete wall that framed the parking, realizing that it was a fairly good spot to look into the bar. Did it mean anything? She went a bit further up the small slope, almost stepping onto a piece of paper. Bending down, Ellie realized it was a flyer, part of it torn off, from a firm renting out storage units. She stood, indecisive for a moment, before she took out a paper tissue and picked up the paper with it. The address part was still visible. It might be a long shot, but Ellie was willing to risk it.

At the storage company, she found a lonely employee playing a video game on this phone. He looked doubtful when she asked about Hogan. Ellie had to admit she'd have doubts too.

"I don't know if I can give you that information. Can't you get a warrant?"

"That might take a while. Mr. Hogan is currently in a complicated surgery after getting shot, and he might not survive. The sooner we can find the shooter, the better, wouldn't you say? The incident happened not far from here."

Once she'd mention a shooter, the young man sat up straight.

"You think the person is still in the area?"

"We are looking for them. So, about Mr. Hogan..."

"He's been renting a unit here for over a year. I'll show you, but don't touch anything, okay?"

"I promise. If there's anything that needs further investigation, I'll get you that warrant. I'd just like to take a look."

Ellie suppressed a relieved sigh when the man motioned for her to follow him. They walked along a long corridor, units left and right.

"How long have you been here?" she asked.

"Me? About a year, but the company opened before that. I think Mr. Hogan rented his unit not long after that."

"Okay. Thank you."

Valerie was probably home already. If Ellie's instincts didn't betray her, she'd have to contact her to get the ball rolling. There was something odd about how clean Hogan's apartment had been, even with the tenant who had left after the cabin burned down. No connection to the Randalls, or the white supremacist groups. Had either one of them set him up?

However, when the employee opened the storage unit, every doubt she'd had regarding the stalking, vanished. The inside was practically wallpapered with pictures of Elizabeth Randall, recent, and, Ellie assumed, from their time in Caton. In none of these pictures she looked directly into the camera.

"Holy shit."

She looked down at the boxes, some open, and stepped back out. "I'm going to get the warrant, don't worry."

Chapter Nine

While they waited, the young employee offered her a coffee which Ellie didn't turn down. Finally, Valerie came through and she could get back into the storage unit. There were more photographs. It might be true that Hogan never talked to Elizabeth Randall, while they lived in Caton, or after they'd moved here. In any case, he seemed to have barely taken his eyes off her. Pictures showed her in front of her workplace, out on her balcony, even on pictures shot through her kitchen window.

"I had no idea."

"Don't worry," she said absent-mindedly. "You're not under suspicion of anything. By the way, could you check your records for a Brad Sellers?"

"That your suspect?"

"Just something I'd like to check."

"Okay. I'll be right back."

With gloved hands, Ellie opened another box that contained women's clothes. Had Hogan stolen them from Elizabeth, or had he bought them—kept for a specific purpose? If he survived the shooting, there was no way he'd get out of this.

She wondered if Maria had gotten anything out of Randall.

"All right, we can rule him out as the shooter. Randall has an alibi. Wait, what's that?" Maria asked, indicating the opened gift basket.

"That's how you should treat your colleagues," Jordan returned, not sure whether she should be amused or slightly annoyed with everyone's reaction. "Okay. Sorry. Don't make that face. Help yourself."

Maria sighed. "I love you. Thanks."

"So, Randall, any chance he could have hired someone?"

"There's always the chance. I'll do some more digging. But based on what I know about him, I'd say if he wanted to kill Hogan, he'd walk up to him and do it. These are expensive. Someone must really owe you."

"Could you give it a rest already? It's chocolate. Excuse me," she said when her cell phone rang. "Carpenter."

"Hey, it's me."

Ellie sounded tired.

"Hey." Jordan softened her tone. "Anything new?"

"I'll be back soon. We definitely have tons of proof for the stalking, but I'm worried Hogan isn't going to be held accountable for it. He might not make it."

"Okay." Likely, that wasn't the reaction Ellie had hoped for, but the day just kept dragging on, and all the tea and chocolate in the world didn't change the fact that she was ready for a break. "I guess we'll have to wait until tomorrow. We are still going over documents. Hogan donated quite a bit to far-right groups, and he was also active in at least one of them that met regularly at the bar. Sellers was present too, but there's nothing illegal—yet."

"So, she was kidnapped and murdered by a neo-Nazi—sympathizer, at best, and we might just have to close the file."

"Unless we can prove those guys intimidated people in town or committed other crimes, I'm afraid we might."

"This sucks," Ellie said with emphasis. "All right. I'm coming home."

"Yes, please. Let's call it a day."

⁕

Jordan had packed up the rest of the chocolates and driven home, expecting Ellie in a little over ninety minutes. At home, she prepared a salad and considered a relaxing bath, when the doorbell rang. For a moment, she entertained the idea of not answering. Ellie had a key, and there was no way she could have made it here so quickly.

It could be Shriver checking on how his gift had been received. She wasn't in the mood. The bell rang again, and with a sigh of the long-suffering, Jordan went to open the door.

She had not expected who was on the other side of that door. From what she could tell, the other person was experiencing just as much of a surprise.

"Jordan," Bethany said.

Jordan had never seen her this dumbfounded. She could only guess the reason.

"Hey. Bethany. What brings you here?" She decided to go with polite small talk for now.

"I won't be long. I suspected that you'd be home by now, and I wanted to talk to you before tomorrow."

"All right. Come on in."

In the years they'd been together, many things had been left unspoken, but Jordan could always tell one thing for certain: She knew when Bethany didn't approve. Bethany didn't approve of what she was seeing, not that Jordan cared. She didn't want to know the reasons either. That would only mean poking at uncomfortable subjects. If they hadn't done well addressing them as a couple, they sure wouldn't be able to do so as friends.

"Ellie will be home in an hour or so."

"Yeah, I don't think I'll bother you that long."

They sat down in the living room, and Bethany, who had never been here, took a curious look around. Jordan wanted to be friendly, but she wasn't going to give her a tour.

"Okay. How can I help you?"

Bethany shook her head with a smile.

"No, this is just a friendly heads-up. When I heard Sellers was involved, I asked to be assigned to the case. Now that your suspect is a person of interest to us, we'll need all the documents from the bar. You can wrap up your stalking/kidnapping case."

"Wait. Our stalker/kidnapper is currently in the hospital after someone tried to kill him."

"Yes, and that's not your jurisdiction anymore. Like I said, just a heads-up."

"Well...Okay then. Thanks." Ellie would not be happy about this.

"You're welcome." Bethany hesitated long enough for the silence between them to get awkward. "Congratulations, by the way."

"Thank you."

"I guess I shouldn't be surprised. You guys tried really hard to adopt the girl from the cult. I just didn't realize..."

She didn't finish the sentence, but wasn't leaving either, so Jordan felt obliged to ask, "What?"

"Do you have regrets? That we stayed together this long? I didn't even know that you wanted to have a baby—I was always under the impression that you weren't interested. All of this might have happened sooner for you."

"It's happening now, and I'm happy and grateful for everything the way it is." Every dysfunctional aspect of her relationship with Bethany made her appreciate her life with Ellie so much more. Jordan kept that summary to herself, knowing it would be only cruel to share—besides, she was aware of how much she had contributed to that dysfunction.

"I'm happy for you then. I should go. Tomorrow's going to be a big day."

"Sure. Have a good night."

Jordan got up to walk her to the door. Halfway, Bethany turned around so abruptly they almost collided.

"I do have regrets," Bethany said. "Many. Everything you did, there was a reason for it. I gave you a lot of reasons."

"I don't want to do this." Now—or ever.

"No, hear me out, because I won't ever mention it again, but this is important. You really were the love of my life."

For a few seconds, Jordan wondered if she had been drinking. Bethany rarely had more than a glass of wine or a beer, but she found her behavior disconcerting. That would have been Jordan, back in the day, making an ill-timed alcohol-fueled confession.

"It's over and done, I know. I thought you should know. And now that I've embarrassed myself appropriately, I'm going to call it a night. I'll see you tomorrow at the department."

"Yeah. Drive carefully." It was a bit of a cop-out, but it was all Jordan could come up with at the moment. She couldn't wait for Ellie to come home. Most of this day had been too bizarre.

*

Over a late dinner, they shared findings and events of the day, after Ellie had finally made it home. She, too, found the gift basket a strange but welcome idea. After seeing some of the documents seized at the bar, she didn't think it was surprising that the FBI was looking into Sellers once more. She was only mildly irritated with Bethany's revelation the day before they'd have to meet with her in a professional context again.

"Her timing is something, as usual, but I don't think I can even have an opinion right now."

"I don't know what this was all about. I didn't want to keep anything from you."

"I know. It's just...kind of typical."

Jordan's expression told her she knew exactly what Ellie meant.

"It is, along with the 'we're coming in and taking over your case.' Part of me is relieved though. It's out of our hands."

"Yeah." There might be the sliver of a chance to get a bit more out of Hogan before the FBI got their hands on him. If that was the case, Ellie would take it. She didn't want Jordan to worry, but if she could get anything else out of him, something to give Matt Randall closure, it would be worth the risk.

⁂

Ellie stole out of the house when Jordan was still fast asleep, after leaving a note on the coffeemaker she'd prepared. *Had an errand to run, see you at work Love you, E.* That didn't sound too suspicious, did it? It seemed wrong that Hogan might be slipping away without ever admitting to any wrongdoing, even if all the papers and photos from the storage locker told a different story. There had to be something more, something definitive. And she had to find it before the FBI got there.

At the hospital, Ellie flashed her badge and asked to speak to the surgeon.

"He's not here today," the receptionist told her. "Perhaps you could come back this afternoon?"

"I'm sorry, that won't work. I need to see Mr. Robert Hogan."

"Detective," someone said behind her, and she turned around to recognize the intern she'd spoken to the other day. "Harding, it is, right?"

"Yes. Dr. Grayson, I need to see Mr. Hogan. It's urgent."

She could tell the doctor had doubts before she spoke. "Dr. Martin isn't here right now, and I don't know..."

"Please. It's important."

"He's awake, but still very much out of it. I'm not sure what you're hoping to find."

"We suspect Mr. Hogan stalked a woman for years, then kidnapped and murdered her." Ellie kept her voice low, so no one but the doctor could hear her. The woman's eyes widened. "Can I see him?"

"I guess you can have a few minutes. Please follow me."

Hogan looked deathly pale, but the corners of his mouth turned upwards when he saw Ellie.

"Did you find...the bastard who shot me?"

"I was hoping you could tell me who did?"

With some difficulty, he shook his head.

"Didn't see him. Perhaps...the husband."

She wasn't going to waste time explaining Randall's alibi to him.

"How did Elizabeth Randall die? Did you kill her? Did she fall trying to get away from you?"

Dr. Grayson still stood by the door. She made no move to interrupt Ellie.

"Aren't you going to arrest him? She loved me."

"Keeping somebody against their will isn't love."

"You have no idea what real love is—"

Ellie could sense his anger, even though his voice was still weak. He coughed.

"Mr. Hogan, we found the storage locker. We found everything. We know what you did."

"You don't know shit!" He coughed again, and Grayson took a step closer. Ellie hold up a hand. "We're almost finished here."

"Then tell me. Make me understand. You might even unburden your conscience, which is probably a good thing given your condition."

"Detective..." Dr. Grayson sounded unsure.

Hogan scoffed. "You don't get it. I didn't want to kill her. I wanted to keep her forever."

Ellie kept her expression impassive as a cold shiver skittered down her spine. Here it was.

"Betty wasn't patient. She tried to run...and fell."

"You're still lying. The wound was too severe. She tried to escape, you hit her."

"I knew you wouldn't get it. She was mine. She was going to love me back."

Ellie had heard enough. She could tell from Dr. Grayson's expression that she was feeling as sick.

"Thank you, Mr. Hogan. And by the way, as soon as you're well enough, you're going straight to jail. Elizabeth Randall loved her husband."

She hadn't heard the door open, so Ellie jumped at the sound of a familiar voice behind her.

"I think that's enough. We'll take it from here."

She turned around to face the music.

"Bethany."

"I thought I'd find you here. We have a lot to talk about."

"I guess so." Ellie thought it was better not to go into details about what she'd learned from Jordan the other night. "We'll take this to the station?"

"Yes, let the hospital staff do their job. We'll deal with him later." Bethany cast a disgusted look at Hogan.

He had fallen back asleep.

Jordan arrived in time for the morning's briefing. Ellie came in a few seconds after the lieutenant, coffee in hand, looking thoughtful. Jordan had wondered about the "errand." She had no doubts it had to do with the FBI taking over the Hogan case.

"I believe you'll have some paperwork to finalize for Dr. Roberts?" Lieutenant Carroll asked Ellie.

"I'll take care of it."

Bethany joined them halfway through. She didn't take a seat but leaned back against the wall instead. A few minutes later, Officer Potts peeked inside after knocking on the door. "Ellie? There's a call for you. Mr. Randall," she added.

Lieutenant Carroll nodded to Ellie, and she got to her feet to leave. When the door was closed again, he addressed Bethany.

"Dr. Roberts, you have something to share."

"Thanks, Lieutenant," she said and walked to the front of the table. "Good morning. As we speak, Mr. Hogan is doing better. Earlier he was able to give a more detailed description of the events at the cabin to Detective Harding. Now, you already know why I'm here. Hogan's connections to Sellers and the gentlemen in his bar prompted us to take a closer look. Above all, I prefer a peaceful transition of power. I don't want to take any resources away from you, but I hope one of you can make the time to bring me up to speed. No heavy lifting involved, I promise," she said with a look to Jordan.

"That's decided, then," Carroll said. "Detective Carpenter will help you with that. Anything else?"

Jordan refrained from rolling her eyes, barely. She hadn't expected to spend the day with Bethany, but it looked like there was no escape.

"All right then. Get to work."

Ellie was gone when they settled in at Jordan's desk.

To her relief, Bethany was all business this morning, listening as Jordan related everything they knew about Hogan and his connections. She leafed through the files and took notes, mentioning neither Jordan's pregnancy nor yesterday's confession.

Halfway through the morning, Detective Shriver walked into the bullpen, halting when he realized Jordan wasn't alone. At least, he hadn't brought any gifts today. Bethany looked up, leaning back in her chair.

"Good morning. Detective...Shriver it is, right?"

He didn't return her smile.

"Dr. Roberts."

Jordan had to admit that the cool greeting made her curious, though she was starting to feel relieved that Shriver wasn't going to be a part of Homicide anytime soon. Granted, Derek wasn't too fond of Bethany either, but that didn't have anything to do with the fact that she was a woman, or successful in her job. Derek's resentment stemmed from one clearly defined issue. Jordan hadn't figured out what Shriver's deal was. He'd been sort of latching onto her, but for all the wrong reasons.

"You know him?" she asked when he was out of earshot.

Bethany shrugged. "The way I know most people around here. Wait, that came out wrong."

"Continue."

"Got a chip on his shoulder, tends to sulk when he doesn't get what he wants. You know the type."

"I don't know. We worked together on a case before—he seemed okay. I'm not so sure anymore."

"What, the guy who bought you chocolate?" Maria teased.

"Now I'm intrigued," Bethany said.

"Good for you. Can we wrap this up now?"

Bethany shoved her notes into a folder, though she made no move to leave. This was going to be a long day.

"I heard you saw Veronica—and before you say anything, this is related to the case. Tell me everything."

Jordan had quite enough of light duty, but there was nowhere to go.

Hogan's words, together with the abundance of evidence from the storage locker told a story about Elizabeth Randall's last moments Ellie didn't want to share with Matt Randall. Still, when he asked to meet her in person, she felt she couldn't say no.

"Thank you for coming," he said after letting her inside. "And I'm sorry for what happened the last time. When I saw him...I just lost it. That was stupid, right?"

"You won't have to worry about any legal consequences. Mr. Hogan has other problems at the moment."

"Yes, your colleague came to see me. She said he was shot..."

"I can't tell you details, but he's in federal custody now. I can assure you he won't get away."

"What does that mean? Is he going to get a deal for turning on someone worse than him?"

Ellie wasn't going to admit that she didn't have all the details either, but the idea bothered her. Bethany hadn't said anything of the kind.

"If he survives, and it looks that way, I believe he's going to stand trial for kidnapping and murdering Elizabeth." Seeing the impact her words had, Ellie added, "I'm so sorry."

"Thank you. At least you're trying to see this through, unlike the police up there that let him get away with burning down the cabin."

"Why do you think that?"

He shrugged. "Sheriff never even talked to me. I got the impression he doesn't care that much."

"I'm sure that's not true. Again, I'm very sorry."

Ellie had a lot on her mind when she left. She wondered if Bethany was still at the station.

***

Bethany was sitting at Jordan's desk, enjoying a cup of coffee. Given that somewhat messy look of the workspace, she assumed they were far from done.

"Please don't tell me the guy is getting a deal. He admitted that he killed her!"

Jordan looked a tad frustrated, though Ellie couldn't tell if it was because she thought she was out of the loop, or because she couldn't have caffeine.

"What's that about a deal?" she asked, frowning, giving Ellie a hint.

"Relax, both of you," Bethany said. "No one's getting a deal."

"Randall mentioned something about the sheriff. He thinks they were slow-walking the case. It might be grief, but there might be something more to it..."

"Oh, there's more to it. A colleague of mine is currently looking into the sheriff's campaign donations. Ellie, I'm trying to pay you a compliment. Your work will make sure that Hogan doesn't get a deal if he spills dirt on Watkins. And Jordan, good job on involving Veronica, she always comes through." An incoming text message interrupted her speech, and she picked up her phone and got to her feet. "If you'll excuse me. I'll be back to go over the last pile of papers with you."

When she was out of earshot, Jordan cast a thoughtful look after her and said, "I guess that's as close to an apology as we'll get."

"If all those leads go somewhere, I'm willing to forgive," Ellie said. She must have stared at the coffee for a little too long. Jordan sighed.

"Go get yourself one. I know you were up early. I'll survive."

"I love you so much. Be right back." She leaned over to kiss her the moment Bethany returned.

<hr />

She was his.

This was the way it was supposed to be.

Someday soon, she would love him back.

Chapter Ten

Too early in the morning, Jordan's cell phone started vibrating on the bedside table. Ellie reached over her but was too late—Jordan was already awake.

"Really?" she greeted the caller and handed the phone over to Ellie with a sigh.

"Damn, I'm sorry," Derek said. "It's actually you I wanted to talk to—force of habit."

Ellie looked over to the other side of the bed, where Jordan was almost back asleep, and pushed back the cover.

"You're forgiven this one time. What's the matter?"

"Death," he said. "Cleaning crew found a body in a parking lot."

It was still dark outside. Ellie suppressed a yawn and started gathering her clothes. "Text me the address. I'll be right there."

"See you then."

Despite having her sleep interrupted, Ellie felt wide awake. Somewhat excited that she'd be the first call, even if it hadn't quite worked out that way. A bit antsy regarding the end of the Hogan case, though the rest of the investigation fell outside of their jurisdiction. Perhaps that was exactly what was making her antsy, the unexpected dimensions of this case, and the fact that a far-right politician had apparently covered for a stalker and murderer—and vice versa.

However, she had a new mystery on her hands.

Derek met her in a parking space outside the taped area, coffee in hand.

"That's for you. I've had mine," he said.

"Thank you so much. What do we have?"

"Female, Caucasian, early twenties maybe."

On their way across the parking lot, Ellie took a few sips of her coffee and threw the cup into a garbage bin before she followed Derek inside the taped area.

"Cause of death?"

"Take a look," ME Dr. Melissa Adams said. She gave Derek a quick smile, which Ellie found highly inappropriate—both under the circumstances and given that everyone knew he was married to her best friend Kate.

Ellie crouched down next to the body to look at the tell-tale marks around the woman's neck and winced. Not long ago, a suspect in the interrogation room had tried to choke her. Her body still remembered the pain. Unlike her, the woman had had no one come to her help. A few folded bills lay on top of her body, another twenty about a foot away.

"This usually isn't an area for this kind of activity," she said. "He lured her here?"

Wes Martin, one of the officers first on the scene, joined her. "We found fresh tire tracks—someone got away very fast."

"You talked to members of the cleaning crew?"

"Yeah. Two women who came together, their car is over there," he pointed to a red Chevy outside of the taped area. "It's not far from the entrance they use. They saw her right away and called 911."

Ellie tried to interpret Derek's thoughtful look. There might be prints on the money, but they could be too many to get any clue as to who the perpetrator was. She took in the cheap fabric of the woman's clothes—apart from the skirt riding up some, it almost seemed undisturbed. A quick, cold transaction. She held back the shudder.

Nothing to ID her. A quick examination showed that she had nothing on her but the clothes and the money.

"Okay," Ellie said. "Let's find out who she is, and who did this to her."

Ellie and Derek went back in to share their preliminary findings with the lieutenant.

"The autopsy will be later today. We'll wait for the lab and meanwhile try to figure out who she is and how she ended up in that parking lot," Derek explained.

"You do that. Keep me updated."

Outside the lieutenant's office, Detective Shriver hurried past them with barely a greeting. Ellie thought that between Bethany making a belated declaration and him apologizing with chocolates, she was getting irritated with people pretending she didn't exist.

She welcomed the distraction of her phone ringing.

"Harding."

Okay, perhaps her irritation showed a little in her curt greeting, because Derek gave her a curious look.

"This is Ginny. I don't know if you remember me."

It took her a few seconds, but Ellie did indeed remember the young woman she'd met a few months ago. Back then, Ginny had been homeless but trying to find a job. Ellie hoped she'd succeeded.

"Sure, Ginny, how are you?"

"I'm okay. Look, I heard about the woman you found?"

"Yes? You know who she is?"

"I think so. Her name is Alicia. She worked for...someone I knew."

Ellie made the possible connections quickly. "Can you tell me a bit more? A last name?"

"You'd have to ask him, but I have to get ready for my shift now. Can I meet you there? Supreme Burgers, the parking lot?"

"Sure, I'll be there." She ended the call and picked up her keys and coat. "Let's go."

"Something interesting, I assume?" Derek asked as they headed to the parking lot. "Where are we going?"

"Supreme Burgers," Ellie answered. "We might have an ID on Jane Doe."

"All of this in the same sentence sounds both disturbing and hopeful," Derek remarked.

───

"I'm sorry, I don't have much time." Ginny was looking around as if someone might be watching them, but the people in the parking lot were either employees or customers.

"You said you knew who Alicia worked for?" Ellie reminded her.

"Yes, a strip club a couple miles from the mall." She cast an uncertain look at Derek, then added, "I was there for a while. Not long. She stayed. I never knew her last name, but the folks there should be able to help you."

"How did you know it was Alicia?" Derek asked.

She looked even more uncomfortable. Ellie sent him an imploring look, and he shrugged. "I have to check something in the car."

When he was out of earshot, Ellie continued, "Ginny, this is important. We need to find who did this."

"You can't tell him. Chad, the guy who owns the club, she was sort of his girlfriend."

"Sort of." Ellie kept her anger in check, as it wasn't directed at Ginny. She could see the picture unfold, Alicia, working in the strip club, maybe doing more than dance, for her "boyfriend."

"Yeah, but she wanted to save up and get out of the place, so she was meeting this other guy on the side. I'm scared Chad found out about it. I called her, and he answered her phone. He said she hadn't come in to work. When I asked around, I realized no one had seen her."

"What about the other guy?"

"She used to meet him in a parking lot not far from the club. That's all I know, I swear."

"This is very helpful, thank you, Ginny." Ellie briefly touched the young woman's shoulder. "If you can think of anything else, please call."

"You're not going to tell Chad I talked to you?"

"I promise. Before you go...how have you been? You found a job?" Ellie asked, indicating the fast-food restaurant.

"Yes, Meg and I could rent a room together. It's not much, but we're trying to get enough for an apartment."

"That's really great." For a split-second, Ellie had a guilty conscience for getting frustrated over small, inconsequential things earlier. She and Jordan were highly privileged to be able to live the way they did, make the choices they had made.

"Yeah, it is. And I'm really sorry about Alicia, but this can't come back to me. For the first time ever, things are going right."

"I understand. We'll have to go see Chad, but I won't mention you. It will be all right."

"Thank you. I need to go to work now."

Ellie went back to join Derek in the car. "When's the last time you went to a strip club?" she asked.

They stopped for a snack on the way, talking strategy. From what Ginny had told Ellie, it could have been either way. Chad might have committed or commissioned the murder out of jealousy or revenge. The mysterious other man could be their perp. A last name would hopefully turn up a paper trail and more witnesses. And yes, they'd have to visit the strip club though that would open later.

A quick search turned up Chad Warner, owner of *The Velvet Rope*.

"Classy," Derek said. "Any priors?"

"The usual. Assault, extortion, has stayed within the law for the past ten years, on paper, anyway."

"Well, we're going to check that later. Something tells me dancing is not the only thing he has his employees do."

"Yeah." Ellie sighed. "It never ends, does it? I was happy to see that Ginny and Meg made it, but there are too damn many Alicias."

Derek didn't disagree.

They parked on the curb near the entrance of the club, a non-descript concrete building with the business's name in neon lights.

The bouncer gave them a curious look when they approached the door.

"No ladies, sorry. Unless you're here to meet Mr. Warner?"

"Actually, we are," Ellie said, flashing her badge. "Where is he?"

"He's busy. Everything here is in order if that's what you're here for."

"We'd like to talk to him anyway."

With a shrug, he turned around. "Follow me."

As they walked through the place, Ellie did her best trying to keep her head down, something that didn't go unnoticed with Derek.

"It really is your first time," he whispered.

"And what's wrong with that? Wait. You didn't go…"

"With Jordan? No. Another case when I was still in uniform. I can't speak for her though."

"You're enjoying this way too much for someone who's married to my best friend," Ellie mumbled.

Derek was about to respond to the charge, but the bouncer stopped abruptly in front of what looked like a fire safety door.

"Chad! The cops are here. They want to talk to you."

A few moments later, the door was opened to reveal Chad Warner, and behind him, a surprisingly huge office space.

"Come on in, officers," he said. "What can I help you with today?"

The bouncer rolled his eyes and walked away.

"I'm sorry about that," Warner said. "My brother. He gets a bit jumpy sometimes, but I guess it comes with the job."

"I'm Detective Henderson, this is Detective Harding. We're here about Alicia."

He gave them a quizzical look.

"Alicia? I hope this isn't bad news? You busted her for possession? I'm afraid I did what I could, gave her a steady job, and a place to live—"

"Mr. Warner!" Ellie interrupted him, holding up her cell phone. "Is this Alicia?"

His face remained impassive, a contrast to his words.

"Oh my God. She's not dead, is she?"

"I'm afraid so. Can you give us a last name? You have an employee file?"

"Alicia was more than that to me, but yes, I do have some papers. Give me a second." He turned around to walk to a filing cabinet, opened it, and hesitated.

For a moment, Ellie felt nervous, her hand going to her gun. Then Warner turned around, file in hand.

"Alicia came to me a couple of years ago. She was a mess. I helped her get straightened out, but sadly, I see that didn't work out in the end."

"Why do you say that?"

"That's obvious, isn't it? What do you think she was doing in that parking lot? It's not safe for the girls to go out there on their own. Too many weirdos."

"And you protect your girls?" Derek said, not trying to hide the sarcasm in his tone.

"Not what you think, Detective. Everything that happens in here is legal, but yes, I protect my employees. We have security to make sure no one harasses them."

Ellie would have thought that having to be naked in the presence of drooling men already qualified as being harassed, but she kept her thoughts to herself. This was about Alicia. They could always check up on Chad Warner's claims. It hadn't gone unnoticed with her that he didn't seem much disturbed by her death.

"Did Alicia have any problems with any client recently?"

"Not that I can think of. She didn't mention anything to me, but then it seems she kept more than that from me. How did she die? Let me rephrase that. What did she overdose on? What a disappointment."

"She was strangled to death," Derek informed him. "We're going to need the footage from your security camera for the past 72 hours."

"And I'm sure you have a warrant."

"I can get one in a few minutes, but I thought you'd want to know who killed her. A murderer sneaking around, that's got to scare off both employees and clients."

Warner gave a dramatic sigh. "Whatever. I have nothing to hide, and if it means I can get you out of here sooner, so be it."

Bethany spent another morning at the precinct.

"We're almost done here," she said, making Jordan worry that she might be too transparent.

"Whatever you need."

"I think we got a lot more than we bargained for already. It's always a pleasure to work with this precinct. The storage locker finished off your case, and this stuff ties Hogan to Sellers and Sheriff Watkins' campaign. I couldn't be happier."

"Great. I'm glad it worked out that way. He needs to go away."

"I agree. Don't you ever feel like you want to sell all your belongings and go live on an island rather than chase women-hating losers?"

Nothing was ever simple small talk with Bethany.

"No," Jordan said. "I find immense satisfaction in putting them behind bars." She harbored the hope that Ellie and Derek might get back to her with something important that would require her to immediately stop traveling down memory lane with her ex. To her disappointment that call never came. Bethany made no move to leave.

"Veronica and Greg still live in town? I might have to visit them too."

"You do that. I'm sure they'll appreciate you checking in with them."

"I think they will, for various reasons. Those folks in that bar give everyone a bad name. Everything that helps to get Sellers and close it down for good."

"Good luck with that." Jordan could only imagine that politics would make this more complicated, but perhaps they'd find enough health code violations to shut them down.

"Taylor still speaks fondly of them—and you, by the way."

When Jordan didn't take the bait, she continued, "Look, I'm sorry I came at this all wrong. I was just so surprised...and I might have had a proposition for you. Taylor is working for a specialized unit now, and they are always looking for good people. I thought that might be right up your alley, but obviously you are determined to put down roots here."

Jordan resented the implied suggestion that her recent choices, home ownership, marriage and motherhood, did anything to hold her back in her career. Come to think of it, Bethany had always felt like she should have a say in it. When she pushed Jordan to get into Homicide—that had been a good idea at the time. That wasn't to say all of her ideas were good ones.

"You don't think that's a good thing."

"I think Ellie is extremely lucky. But if you ever get bored around here, give me a call and I'll hook you up with Taylor. Strictly professionally speaking, of course."

"Yeah, I appreciate your efforts, but that's not likely. If you'll excuse me now..." This was the perfect timing for a bathroom break. Against all reason, Jordan hoped Bethany might be gone when she returned.

He'd been sitting at the desk for almost ten minutes, unfolding paperclips one by one. He picked up one of them, piercing the palm of his hand. The pain did nothing to staunch the flow of memories. He suppressed a curse and reached for a paper towel, about to head for the bathroom when he heard a voice call his name.

He ignored it and kept walking, hearing the sound of a door being slammed in frustration.

They had no idea what frustration meant, never getting what you deserved.

One day, he would show them all, like he had with the hooker. He laughed grimly to himself, ignoring the strange look of a co-worker passing him by in the hallway.

One day.

Chapter Eleven

A licia Fox had lived in a run-down apartment complex not far from the mall where she'd been found. If she had met her client there, she could have gone on foot. Someone might have seen her.

There was an "out of order" sticker slapped onto the elevator, so Ellie and Derek took the stairs up to the third floor. Warner had provided them with an extra key he kept, for emergencies he'd told them. More likely, he had checked up on her on a regular basis. Jealousy might be a motive, but Ellie wasn't willing to rule out the last client yet.

They stepped inside the modest apartment, the sights greeting them confirming the impression they'd had from the outside. If Alicia was seeing clients on the side, she sure hadn't made a lot of money that way.

The kitchen didn't turn up anything out of the ordinary. Ellie opened a cabinet door, finding nothing but mismatched dishes, a few utensils in the drawers. She went to the living room next while Derek checked the bedroom.

A comforter was thrown over one side of the couch, a couple of coasters and a magazine on the coffee table.

Ellie bent to open a drawer that was filled with papers. She picked up a few with a gloved hand, realizing there were bank statements in the mix. One was as recent as last month. When she looked at the number, Ellie thought for a moment that she must have been mistaken.

"Derek? Can you come here for a moment?"

"What is it?"

"Come, look at these. It's unreal."

Derek whistled when he looked at the statements. "What are the odds that Warner didn't know about this?"

"Maybe he just found out and wasn't happy that Alicia was hiding this kind of money from him...but where did she get it from? I found three transfers, all around the same amount, four weeks in between."

"Mystery client?"

"This was not for services rendered," Ellie said. "If she was blackmailing the guy, there's your motive."

"I could see that," Derek admitted, "but let's not rule out Warner just yet."

"I wouldn't dare. We'll take a more in depth look at those tomorrow?"

"Sure. Let's wrap this up."

❧

Ellie found Jordan still at her desk, ready to go home. During the drive, Ellie talked about her day and the recent, curious findings.

"I'm with you," Jordan said. "Warner is probably too exposed with his business. He might not have treated her okay, but she'd be worth more to him alive."

"Except if he thought she was cheating on him. He murdered her in revenge?" Ellie mused. "Did you finish things up with Bethany?"

"Oh yes. She's nothing if not thorough. She also offered me a job she knew I'd never take."

"Really. What kind of job?"

"A new unit far from where I want to be. I didn't ask for details. Wait...why are you stopping?" she asked when Ellie parked in the lot of the fast-food restaurant.

"I thought we could eat something on the way? You must be hungry too?"

Jordan's expression was slightly pained. "To be honest, I'm not. I've been feeling queasy all day, and I'm so tired. Can we just go home? You could get something to go."

"Are you all right?"

"I just need to get some sleep. I'll be okay. I'll wait here."

"Oh no, I can throw something together at home. I'm sorry."

"Don't be." Jordan touched her arm gently, and Ellie pulled out of the parking space and back onto the road.

"You're sure you don't need anything else? Should we stop by the pharmacy?" Ellie would freely admit that as excited she was about this stage in their lives, she was well aware that only one of them was going through a particular experience—and Jordan had a tendency to avoid any subject that could make Ellie worry. Or worry more.

"Home. Please."

"Okay. I got it."

They'd have to do some grocery shopping someday soon, Ellie reflected as she stood in front of the open fridge. Finally, she opted for a PB & Jelly sandwich and a glass of milk. On second thought, she took out the jar of pickles as well and laid one on the side.

"Someone might think you're the pregnant one." Jordan, who had returned from the bathroom, chuckled. She was now clad in a robe that didn't quite close over her belly. "I think I'm the one who should be sorry. That's your dinner?"

"If it can be breakfast, it can be dinner," Ellie returned. "I was going to write down some notes. I think I'll join you soon."

"Okay. See you in a bit." They shared a kiss, and Ellie went back to her sandwich and notebook, trying to make sense of what she'd seen the past days. The crime scene, Alicia's lover—or employer? Pimp?—the old run-down apartment, and the statements showing Alicia Fox was a lot better off financially than one might expect.

Where did that money come from? Ellie didn't think Alicia would be able to have any number of clients without Chad Warner noticing. A man like him was likely to keep tabs on her, either himself or through one of his associates. But in that case, he'd be aware if she slept with anyone else, for whatever reasons? Had he ordered the killing?

Back to the mysterious client. She was certain that he had some answers for them.

Ellie washed her plate and after watching the news, got ready for bed. Jordan was right—no reason to worry. She hadn't gotten much rest lately, and the lack of sleep was likely catching up with her. When Ellie went into the bedroom, she could see that Jordan was catching up on it now, fast asleep under the covers. Ellie was more than happy to join her.

When she woke again, the numbers on the digital clock told her that it was close to two a.m., and she happily drew the sheets higher.

"You're awake?"

Jordan's soft whisper made her sit up, wide awake in an instant.

"Is everything okay? You need anything?" It couldn't be. It was much too early.

"Honestly? I'd love to have that burger now. I'm so hungry."

Ellie took a deep breath in relief. Meri didn't want to come into the world yet. All else they could deal with.

"I could make you a sandwich quick?"

Jordan, however, was taking her time. "Or we could head over to that new 24/7 diner. You didn't have a real dinner either. Their fries are beyond."

Ellie yawned, trying to come to terms with the fact that she was not dreaming.

"You know I love you, but I just want to make sure I got this right. You want us to get up and get dressed, go to the diner, and have burgers and fries at 2 a.m."

"I love you too, and that sounds amazing."

"All right then. Let's do it."

Shivering, Ellie dressed into pants and sweatshirt, extra warm socks. She still didn't feel entirely awake, though Jordan seemed happy to be up and about now. Looking at each other, they both had to laugh.

"This is crazy, right?"

"How much do you want those fries?"

"I can't even begin to tell you."

The next challenge presented itself when they arrived at the counter, and Jordan had trouble deciding what she wanted. Or, more precisely, how to limit herself.

"Look, I'll just have a coffee and a danish," Ellie said. "You get the fries and the onion rings, and we'll go from there."

Jordan cast her a grateful look. "Thank you so much. At this point I feel like I'm possessed."

"No, I don't think so. You've had an appreciation for this kind of food as long as I've known you."

"Yeah, let's not discuss this right here and now."

The bright lighting and strong coffee finally woke Ellie for good, and she couldn't help thinking of how crazy lucky they were. To have found each other, to be able to do what they were

113

doing. A few hours ago, she had stood in the apartment of a dead woman, who didn't have so many options, and might have died trying to create some, any, for herself.

She needed to find that client.

She needed to be in this strange, wonderful moment with her wife who had currently succumbed to pregnancy cravings. Ellie stole a fry off her plate which went surprisingly well with the cherry danish she'd ordered.

"Wow, this is good together."

"I'm definitely not the only one with odd cravings."

"You're right," Ellie said, amused, and snatched another fry before she took a sip of coffee.

"Okay, I'm sorry I wasn't listening much earlier," Jordan admitted. Tell me more about the case." Of course, her wife was also a Homicide detective. "And stop stealing my fries."

"I thought it was implied that we'd share? I'll buy you more if necessary."

"You better," Jordan said, laughing. "Now, about the case."

Ellie was in the middle of relating the latest findings when Officer Sam Potts walked in, her eyes widening when she saw what was on Jordan and Ellie's table.

"Hey. You guys are getting an early start."

"You could say that," Ellie agreed, hiding another yawn behind her hand. "This baby isn't even here yet, and she's giving us an interesting schedule. You want to sit with us?"

"Sure. I'll just get myself some breakfast." She went over to the counter to order.

"Really, my bet is on the client," Jordan said. "I've dealt with Warner before. He's an asshole, but I don't think murder is in his wheelhouse. And he's all about business—if anything, he might have been in on the blackmail, anything for the bottom line."

"Yeah, if only we could figure out who that is."

"Have you looked at the security cameras in the area?" Jordan asked when Sam sat back down at the table.

"We're at it. Hopefully, something helpful will turn up."

"You're coming to roll call this morning?" Sam asked. "If you need any more help with those tapes, I'm sure Sergeant Bristol won't mind."

"Sounds like a good idea." Ellie was aware of Jordan's amused gaze, and the memories this conversation brought up for both of them. Sam had ambitions, no doubt, but they didn't go further than the job. Back in the days, Ellie had another reason for wanting to work with one particular Homicide detective.

They continued their meal for a bit before Sam changed the subject. "So how are you doing? Both of you?"

"Well, she's awake and kicking." Jordan paused for a second, before she continued. "Right now, actually. Would you like to feel?"

Having watched Jordan's frustration over people stepping over her every boundary in the past few months, Ellie still wasn't surprised. Sam was part of their tightly knit chosen family.

Her expression was one of awe.

Chapter Twelve

A fter a few more hours of watching security footage, Ellie did find something, but it was a lot more disturbing than she could have imagined. Her heart was pounding when she knocked on the door of Lieutenant Carroll's office. She had a feeling that this was an urgent matter, but she wasn't being paid to follow a hunch. She needed to make a case, and she couldn't sound like a jealous spouse while trying.

"Come on in!" Carroll called.

After closing the door behind herself, she approached his desk hesitantly.

"I was hoping you had a moment."

Why did it have to be her? Carroll sure hadn't forgotten that her testimony had led to a former colleague's firing. Justified, of course, because Waters had assaulted a young officer—she hoped this would be different. It would also be more delicate, because they'd have to involve another precinct.

"Sure. Please, take a seat. What's the matter?"

"It's about Alicia Fox. We found this."

She handed him the tablet showing the murdered woman on the day of her death, arguing with a familiar figure. The lieutenant recognized him right away, too, she could tell from his changing expression.

"What should we do next?" she asked. Ellie had some ideas, but she didn't want to do anything her boss hadn't signed up on. She couldn't help thinking that this man had sent Jordan expensive chocolates, when he knew that she was married, expecting a baby. It was only natural to be alarmed when the same man had neglected to tell anyone he'd known a woman who had ended up dead not long after he met her.

"For now, treat him as you would any witness. Go talk to him, find out what he knows. I'll keep an eye on the situation, but it might be harmless."

"They're arguing. Now she's dead."

"I'm aware, Harding. You find him, talk to him, and get back to me right away."

"Yes, sir. Should I tell Lieutenant Daniels?"

"There might be nothing to tell. See what you can find out, and I'll talk to her."

Carroll's concerned but calm demeanor helped some with her inner turmoil. Ellie sent a text to Jordan asking her about her impression of Shriver, and if she could think of any red flags. Next, she was on her way to Major Crimes.

She identified herself to an officer at the front desk.

"I'm sorry, Detective Shriver isn't here. He's out on a witness interview." Checking his watch, the officer concluded, "He should be here within the next fifteen minutes, if you want to wait?"

"Yes, thank you." Ellie took a seat in the small waiting area. She hoped that Lieutenant Daniels wouldn't come around to ask her about her business here.

The more she thought about it, the more she might have overreacted, but it never harmed to be sure. Her mind wandered back to the evening Jordan had listened to a drunk and rambling Shriver. He knew that she wasn't going to drink with him. She wasn't available for whatever else might have been on his mind.

Why had he sought her out?

Why did he meet with Alicia Fox?

The truth was, he might have a strange relationship with women—that didn't make him a murderer. She didn't want to think this about a fellow cop, except another fellow cop had revealed himself as a predator. An officer she'd met right out of the academy had threatened her with withholding backup because she hadn't stayed silent. Black sheep, squeaky wheel, both of them, for sure.

Ellie just wasn't certain about Detective Shriver.

To her dismay, she saw Lieutenant Daniels heading straight for her.

"Detective Harding, nice to see you. What can we help you with?"

"I'm waiting for Detective Shriver. I was told he'd be back soon."

"And here he is. Have a good day and give Detective Carpenter my best. When's the big date?"

"November 15th...still a few weeks away."

Shriver stood to the side, his expression slightly impatient, Ellie noticed. She didn't even wonder why Daniels knew. News traveled fast.

"Tell her to hang in there. See you, Detective."

"Yes, thank you."

"You wanted to talk to me?" Shriver asked.

"Yes. Can we go somewhere more private?"

He shrugged, as if unaware of the subject matter she needed to address. "Come with me." He led her down the hall and into a briefing room where he gestured for her to sit down. Shriver remained standing, arms crossed over his chest. "I don't have a lot of time."

"This won't take long. You know Alicia Fox?"

"I'm not sure, why?"

"That's her...and you. Could you tell me what I'm seeing here?"

He let out a quick, incredulous laugh.

"That's it? I told her I was going to bust her for prostitution if she didn't leave—again. She wasn't happy about it."

"What we see here on camera, that's all the interaction you had that day?"

"What the hell? Why would I have any other interaction with her? What are you insinuating?"

"Nothing. You know that she is dead?"

"Well, that's too bad. There are always turf wars, and sometimes, these women get caught in the middle."

Ellie didn't like the way he'd said "these women" at all. Overreacting? She wasn't so sure.

"Any names you can think of that might help me find who did it?"

"I'm sure you checked out Warner. Officially he runs the strip club, but he still has business on the side. He's usually very careful about that, but as I said. Someone else might have wanted a piece of the pie."

She tried hard not to shudder. "So, you didn't know her name?"

"I told you, Harding. I need to go back to work. Is that all?"

"For now. Please let me know if you can think of anything else."

Part of her wanted to ask him what he'd been thinking sending her wife chocolates. Maybe it really was the clumsy apology they had taken it for.

She couldn't become paranoid.

"Thank you. I appreciate you making time for me."

"It's no problem," he said. "Say hello to Jordan for me."

At the very least, Ellie didn't like him. But she had an idea where to go next.

At the *The Velvet Rope*, she asked to see Chad Warner, whose brother/bouncer led her to the office once more.

"Detective," he said, getting up from behind his desk to greet her. "I take it you have news on Alicia?"

"Possibly. Did you ever see this man at the club?" She held out her phone to him.

"I'll be damned." Chad Warner whistled through his teeth as he studied the photo. "Is that the guy who killed her? I told her she couldn't trust a pretty face. They always have something to hide."

"Slow down, Mr. Warner, we're not there yet," Ellie warned him. "You recognize him?"

"Damn well, yes I do. He comes here at least every other week. Not your boyfriend, is he?" he added when Ellie had a hard time hiding her surprise. She would have expected Shriver to be a lot more discreet, if he'd met Alicia on a regular basis. Maybe she was going at this all wrong. Could he be working undercover? In that case, why wouldn't he be more motivated to help Ellie find Alicia's killer?

But both could be true, he could have been undercover and crossed some lines along the way.

"Not the point, but maybe you could tell me a bit more about him." She had to be careful too—if her work was jeopardizing that of another cop, she could be in trouble soon. Ellie wondered if Carroll's careful approach meant that he knew more than she did? But he wouldn't set her up to fail.

"Pretty easygoing, has a few drinks, watches the girls, goes home. Honestly, I don't see him killing anyone. Doesn't seem like the type."

Ellie could have told him that she'd come across plenty of people that didn't seem like "the type" to kill another person and had anyway. Instead, she said, "So no problems, with any of the girls, or Alicia?"

"Not that I know of, but how many times are you going to ask me that question?"

"That's it for now. Thank you, Mr. Warner."

Ellie left the club and went back to her car, not much the wiser. What was Shriver's deal with Alicia? If she'd been an informant for him, this couldn't be where the money came from, not these sums. Had he tried to get her out, maybe even imagined a future with her? It didn't look like Alicia had planned to go anywhere.

She might be reading the signs wrong. The only way they could figure this out was if they kept closer tabs on Shriver, but it would be hard to convince a D.A. to sign off on surveillance of another cop—at least where the case stood now. Ellie knew she needed more.

Lost in thought, she jumped at the rap against the driver's window. She didn't recognize the woman, but judging from the attire that peaked out from under her coat, Ellie assumed that she worked in the club.

"Can I get in?" she asked, shivering.

Ellie opened the door on the passenger side, and the woman climbed into the seat, taking a deep breath. "I hear you're asking about that guy. The cop?"

"Do you have any information?"

"Chad doesn't know, but Alicia told me that she'd been meeting him in a parking lot for the past three, four months. You do the math."

"Did she mention anything about money?"

"Lady, she was about to buy herself a new ID and get out of this place. She didn't give me any numbers, but apparently, he paid well. Or she made him, I don't know."

"Why didn't you talk to the police before? We were looking for Alicia's client!"

"Well, you found him without me, and no one ever asked me. I didn't even know it was all about him until you showed that picture to Chad. And he's going to have my hide if I don't go back in now."

"Wait. What's your name?"

"Janine. It's better if you don't talk to me again. I don't want to end up like Alicia." She sighed, and added, "Meg said you were okay. I didn't even want to say anything in case you closed ranks around him. Not that it would be the first time."

"Is that all she said?" Ellie didn't want to make any promises at this time, though she was grateful for Meg putting out the word. It was necessary to have the people they served trust them, though everyone had waited too long to move in Waters' case. If he had behaved with witnesses the way he had around colleagues, Ellie didn't want to imagine what else could have happened.

"She said he had kinky tastes. Make of that what you will, kinky is pretty relative around here. Have a good day."

"Janine! Would you come with me and make an official statement?"

"Not asking for much, are you? I need to go back in there. You know what they say about looking a gift horse in the mouth. Don't. Have a good day, Officer."

Ellie's mind was on too many things for her to correct Janine on her rank. She decided to head back to the station and bring her findings to the lieutenant.

At the precinct, she knocked on the door of his office and walked inside, halting in her tracks. Ellie had not expected for things to move this fast. Lieutenant Daniels was sitting in Carroll's office, looking concerned.

"I'm sorry," Ellie said. "I'll come back later."

"No, please, have a seat," Carroll said. "If there's anything new, you can tell me in front of Lieutenant Daniels since this concerns her too."

Her body language revealed without a doubt how unhappy Daniels was with the situation, but she nodded. "Go ahead, Detective."

After listening to Ellie relate the conversation she'd had with Janine, she shook her head. "I don't like this. Of course, I can't look away when there's unethical behavior from one of my detectives. You can be sure there will be consequences. I'd hate to find out there's even more."

"We don't know that for sure yet," Carroll reminded her. "If there was a connection to the payments made to Alicia Fox, that would be pretty damning."

"What a nightmare," Daniels said. "I looked into Noah's case files, and he had reasons to be around Warner more than once. We need to bring in your witness for a statement. Tell her and Warner that she is not in trouble."

"We'll have to bring in Detective Shriver as well, hear a bit more about his side of the story," Carroll added.

"Of course."

"First thing tomorrow morning. Harding, I'll expect you here at seven."

"Yes, sir."

"I'll give a heads-up to A.D.A. Esposito. I'll see you all tomorrow then."

"Unfortunately," Lieutenant Daniels muttered.

Ellie could tell Carroll was sympathetic, but there was no way around identifying the bad apples. Shriver might not have murdered Alicia—and part of her still hoped he hadn't—but he had tarnished his profession all the same. There was no getting away from that.

Jordan had already left. Ellie decided to call it a day as well and headed home. Over dinner, she could finally update Jordan on the recent events.

"Wow. No. I'm not sure I can deal with this right now. Do I have that much of a knack for attracting psychos? I'm scared for Meri."

Ellie had expected Jordan to be upset, though she hadn't anticipated this reaction.

"Well, you attracted me too—I hope that counts for something."

Jordan wasn't in the mood for reassurances. "That's not what I mean, and you know it. That damn chocolate."

"Relax. We don't know for sure yet. It might be a number of unfortunate coincidences. We'll bring him in tomorrow, clear it all up."

"Hopefully." Jordan sighed. "I want to be there. Maybe it helps. Whatever tomorrow brings, he obviously came to me for a reason."

"You're sure you don't want to sit this one out?" The words were out before Ellie could consider their implications.

"Yes, I'm sure. I've been sitting out everything for weeks now. I think I can handle a bit of talk with Shriver."

"Yeah. Sure. No argument from me. We'll clear it with Carroll and Daniels."

"I'm sorry. I'm just so...ready for something different."

"I understand. I see no reason why you shouldn't talk to him."

Chapter Thirteen

I n the light of day, she saw many reasons not to get too close to him. Jordan stood on the other side of the two-way mirror, watching an angry Noah Shriver fidget in his seat. He was smart, so he wasn't going to lose it completely in there, yet she couldn't fight the shiver running down her spine. She'd gone into much more dangerous situations not even giving it a second thought, but this was different. Meri made all the difference.

She had offered—she wasn't going to back down now. And like her colleagues she believed that she had a good shot at making him talk. Jordan took a deep breath and went into the room.

Noah Shriver's demeanor changed immediately. He sat up straighter, giving her a cordial smile.

"Jordan. I thought you were on desk duty until the baby arrives."

"I am. I just wanted to talk to you."

"Why? It seems that people, including my own boss, have already made up their minds." He shook his head. "No good deed goes unpunished."

"What does that mean? You gave money to Alicia Fox?"

"If you're asking, I guess that means you already know. Yes, damn it, I gave her money. I interviewed her for a case, it's all in my reports. I knew she was in a desperate situation, and I wanted to help her."

"Two payments of 15K? That's a lot of money."

"To make a fresh start. We can't help them all, but I thought I could make a difference."

His tone was calm, eye contact unwavering. He expected her to believe this.

"And, could you? Make a difference? Or did she decide to take the money and stay with Warner anyway?"

"Come on, you know how it goes. He found out and killed her, just to have the last word—and, of course, the money. I won't claim I made a particularly smart decision here, but you know me." His gaze on her was intense, imploring. "You know I didn't kill her."

Jordan was uncomfortably reminded of his questions the night at the *SEVEN*.

"If you suspected that Warner is our guy, why didn't you come forward?"

"I didn't think I had to. Henderson and Harding were already looking at Warner, and I thought they'd be doing a better job. No offense."

"You don't have to apologize to me. You understand why your story still sounds a little off?"

"What the hell do you want me to say?" With a wry smile, he held up his hands. "Relax, guys, I'm not going to touch her," he said to the two-way mirror. "All I ever wanted was to help. Yes, I crossed some lines, and I guess I was too embarrassed to come forward. Warner played me, too. 30K down the drain. I'm not proud of it."

Perhaps they were on to something. He didn't sound so altruistic now.

"Did you try to recover the money from Warner?"

"Yes. He laughed in my face and told me I should write off my losses."

"Because you'd been to the club a few times, and he thought that gave him something to blackmail you?"

"I'm not sure I should tell you anything else without my lawyer and union rep present. Are you charging me with anything?"

"We wanted you to give a chance to clarify things first."

Shriver avoided her gaze now, staring at his hands for long seconds.

"Okay, you got me," he finally said. "It's not exactly an excuse, but I've had a couple of pretty rough years. My wife left me. She stayed in the house we'd bought. I really enjoyed that other time we worked together."

It took Jordan a split-second to realize he was talking about her. Obviously, he had picked up some gossip not long after, but by the time he sent those chocolates for everyone at work to see, he had to have known some facts.

"But you knew I was married."

"I made a fool of myself more than once, didn't I?"

"Noah. This is serious."

For a second, Jordan wondered if it made her a bad person that she almost enjoyed herself. It had been a while since she had the chance to display her skills in the interrogation room, and it was a bit of a rush to realize she wasn't rusty at all. She could tell by the change in his demeanor.

"I understand." He sighed. "I just thought I could catch a bit of a break, you know?" By going off the books to help Alicia, or making a half-hearted pass at a married, pregnant woman? He had to realize how strange that sounded. "I don't know. It all went to hell in the blink of an eye...but I'm telling you, you need to lean on Warner. He runs a tight ship. Alicia wanted to get out, but she was also afraid."

"She had nothing to fear from you."

"Of course not. I liked her. I wanted to help her."

There was a knock on the door, before Ellie peeked inside. "Could you come here for a moment?"

"Excuse me. Would you like a coffee or something?"

"A coffee would be nice. Thank you."

"No problem."

Noah Shriver looked down at his hands again while Jordan got to her feet and left the room to join Ellie and the others in the observation area.

❧

Ellie had to remind herself that they'd talked about this from all angles. The two of them had come up with the concept, and it had been approved by both Carroll and Daniels. Obviously, it was a good idea. It didn't mean that she had to like seeing it in action.

Jordan and Meri were safe with a group of cops on the other side of the two-way window, and clearly, Shriver was too smart to lose it in this context. Nevertheless, he had some troubling issues.

Ellie didn't want Jordan anywhere near him. She breathed a sigh of relief when Jordan followed her outside.

"This is Janine Milner," she said, introducing the dancer from Warner's club she'd met the day before. In the interrogation room, Shriver hadn't moved. He was wound tight, but he understood what was at stake. "Janine, I want you to take your time. Is that the man you saw at the club?"

Janine scoffed. "I don't need to take my time. That's him, for sure. Came every Friday for a while, but he didn't talk to Alicia at the club. I didn't know she was involved with him until she told me about the meetings in the parking lot."

"Did she ever mention any names?" Ellie asked, though she already knew the answer. She wanted the full impact, Janine's statement in the present of both her supervisor, and Shriver's.

"She called him Noah, said he was a cop. I didn't make the connection until you showed me the picture. I swear."

"What about Chad? You seemed afraid of him yesterday."

"He's no choirboy, that's for sure," she said. "But that one," Janine added with a nod to Shriver on the other side of the glass, "he was acting out some crazy fantasies when they met in that parking lot. Choking her and all."

Ellie felt her stomach churn even harder thinking of all the attention he'd given Jordan lately, though Jordan seemed unfazed. Daniels' expression was grim, Carroll's unreadable. Perhaps he was relieved this didn't concern someone in his own precinct.

"Look, Chad can be a mean bastard, but he wants us alive and working. This guy...I don't know. Always well-dressed and polite. For all the money he threw at Alicia, he didn't seem to think much of any of us."

"Thank you, Janine. You've been very helpful."

How ironic and sad that this case could still go either way, the owner of a strip club, a cop, either of them could have killed her on purpose, or accidentally. She thought back to Elizabeth Randall, dead because Hogan thought he owned her. That was how little all of those men had valued the life of a woman. They'd get to the bottom of this either way, and Ellie vowed to make life harder for Chad Warner even if it turned out he wasn't the perp, this time.

"I can go?"

"Yes. Detective Carpenter can see you out while I get the gentleman his coffee."

Both Janine and Jordan seemed amused at the statement, though for different reasons, Ellie assumed. Janine probably appreciated Ellie's sarcastic tone regarding Shriver, while Jordan was not used to having Ellie tell her what to do at work. No one opposed her suggestions though. It was up to her to bring it home now.

⁂

"I didn't know if you wanted milk or sugar, so I brought you both."

The alarm in Shriver's expression was unmistakable. "Where's Jordan?" Before Ellie could answer, he added, "Is she okay? Is it the baby?"

Ellie didn't want him to think about Jordan, or their baby, ever again. She sat across from him and took a sip of her own, black, coffee.

"Jordan is fine, but she had something else to do. Don't worry, this is still just a friendly conversation. We're trying to figure out what happened, all right?"

"I am not so sure of that."

"Look, I'm trying to understand. Obviously, you've been under a lot of stress for some time. I always wanted to be in Homicide, and it wasn't easy."

"Easy enough for you, or so I heard."

"Yeah, don't believe everything you hear. You still want to make friends around here, this is not the way."

"I get the impression that most of you were not interested in making friends outside your exclusive club. Jordan was the only one who cared to listen."

"Well, I'm listening now. You wanted to help Alicia, so you took some unusual steps. That's...partly admirable, but also reckless. In any case, I can see you had good intentions. But something went wrong."

She paused, giving him a chance to explain himself. Shriver didn't take it, holding her gaze with what looked like a smirk to her.

"What did go wrong? You choked her too hard?"

To her surprise, he laughed. "Says who? Warner? He should know about these things."

"No, not Warner. Someone else Alicia confided in, someone credible."

"You're not talking about any of those girls that would say anything for a few dollars? Come on, you're smart, Harding. You know as well as I do that Warner probably told her to say that. He might have promised her something in return or simply threatened her. You want this to be friendly? You are all going quite far accusing a fellow cop. I haven't taken any steps yet because I still think you'll all come to your senses. I hope you will before everyone finds out what this is really about."

"And what would that be?"

"It's convenient, isn't it? Waters is out, then Atwood, which doesn't really shine such a great light on the precinct, but what if someone digs deeper? About how you got your promotion really quick? And Jordan, I like her, but doesn't she have a tendency to go into a dangerous situation without backup? Isn't that what happened with Darby?"

"You are so wrong."

"On all of it? I don't think so. You're too happy to distract from what else has been going on here."

Ellie got up to walk around the table, perching on the edge of it, closer in his personal space. Shriver didn't budge.

"What's been going on here is that a woman is dead. You admitted to giving her money. She told a friend that you met regularly in a parking lot. You liked to choke her. It might have been an accident."

"You are good, Harding, but not that good. Are you charging me? If not, this conversation is over." He leaned forward to whisper. "That friend better be careful making false accusations. They can come back to bite a person."

It occurred to Ellie that while Janine might have been unaware of who Shriver was when he came to the club, the opposite might not be true. They had to make sure she was safe.

"It's okay, you can go now. We'll be in touch."

"Can't wait."

She didn't want to tip him off, so she didn't say what was on her mind. There had better not be any violent adult rated movies on any of his devices. She hoped that if he owned anything like that, he wouldn't have the time to get rid of it.

"Not to sound like creepy Shriver, but aren't you going to stop working soon? You seem...ready?"

Coming from Derek, Jordan knew how to take this question, even on a day that came with many mixed emotions.

"I am. Soon I'll stay home and ponder my lack of intuition when it comes to men. I thought he had some issues...not like that though."

"We all invited him," Derek reminded her. "He's cornered and now wants to shift the blame any way he can. That's on him."

"Sure. Doesn't mean I have to be happy about it. He's going to try and find someone else to blame."

"Likely, but it won't work. Besides, you'll take a break and we'll hopefully be back to normal by the end of it."

"That's optimistic, but I'll take it."

Yes, she was ready for that break. Would it help her to get ready, or give her more time to become terrified, Jordan wasn't sure yet.

In any case, clarity mattered. She hoped they would find it in Shriver's case before it was time for her to fully focus on other matters.

Chapter Fourteen

She had done all she could do for the day. Shriver had huddled with his lawyer and union rep and wouldn't answer any more questions unless they charged him with a crime, knowing full well they didn't have enough on him yet. Officer Potts was with Janine at her apartment.

Ellie wanted to take a break from the day's work, though that might be easier said than done. She was supposed to meet Jordan, Derek, and Kate for dinner, but when she arrived at the *SEVEN*, they had more company than expected. Bethany, and Veronica Sawyer.

Ellie bristled a little, still, at Bethany's confession and her uninvited judgment on Jordan's pregnancy. Veronica's presence didn't bother her that much, though it would have been nice to have a more private, quiet evening with just their closest friends. She stopped at the bar to say hi to Jack, watching the group for a moment. It looked like Bethany was on good terms with Veronica. *Figures.* They all shared some history, the two of them, and Jordan—and the mysterious Taylor Hudson. Nothing mysterious about her, Ellie reminded herself. And she had no reason to be jealous of anyone.

"I'll have a cheeseburger and fries," she told Jack. "Make that double fries, my wife will appreciate even if she has her own."

"No problem," he said, laughing. "Go sit, I'll be right with you."

"Thank you."

She didn't mean to be petty, but why was Bethany even still in town? She wasn't the department's liaison with the FBI anymore, had moved on to another job, which was fine with Ellie. Bethany might be brilliant, something Ellie admired, but whenever she was present, she couldn't help meddling or dropping the occasional jibe. That, Ellie could do without, especially now.

"Hey," she greeted the group before sitting down and whispering to Jordan, "Is this a coincidence or did I miss something?"

Jordan shrugged. "Hell if I know. Did you get extra fries?"

Ellie couldn't help smiling. No, she didn't have any reason to worry.

"Course I did. I know what you like."

That, she didn't whisper, and Kate's amused expression told her she had seen through her.

"You guys are so cute," Bethany commented. "So, it looks like I'm going to be in town for a bit longer. That simple homicide turns out to be a lot more complex than anyone thought."

"What does that mean?" Ellie asked before she could stop herself. "It's not that far-right wing group meeting in the club?"

"Oh, they are up to their necks in it, and that bar is going to be shut down for sure. It is taking longer than I'd like. But what is it I hear about Shriver? I swear that guy's trouble. I hope you got your ducks in a row before bringing him in."

"It wasn't my first time."

Ellie wondered why all other conversations at the table had stopped all of a sudden, and why she'd felt the need to make this about her.

In the midst of this awkward moment, her cell phone rang. Ellie barely refrained herself from sighing in relief—relief that was short-lived, when she realized it was Officer Potts on the phone.

"Excuse me, I have to get that," she said, and answered. "Harding."

"Ellie, thank God. We thought you should hear this right away. Janine wants to leave, and she wants to retract the statement she made."

"What?"

"We could convince her to wait for you, but you have to come right away. I'm really sorry."

"No, don't be, you did the right thing. Keep her there, I'm on my way."

Maybe it wasn't the worst thing that she had to leave the table, though the news troubled her. In building the case against Shriver, Janine's testimony was instrumental. Ellie couldn't have her walk away now. She ended the call and whispered a short summary to Derek. "I'll try to get Esposito on the way."

"You want me to come?"

"No, thanks. I can handle it. I'll see you at home?" she finally addressed Jordan who nodded, her expression somewhere between proud and pensive. Bethany looked amused, Veronica intrigued. Ellie didn't have time to address any of it.

"I honestly meant to be nice," Bethany said, leaning back into the booth, glass in hand. "She's right to take a good hard look at Shriver, you know."

"And you're telling us now. You know something we don't?"

As usual, Derek wasn't holding back when it came to Bethany. Usually, Jordan would have tried to calm things, but at the moment, she was content to sip her iced tea and let her friends talk it out. She'd come to realize that her interventions

139

made little difference, and besides, she had other, more important things to think about. The brief conversation she'd had with Derek earlier reminded her how close she was to being off work for a while, actually, the longest time she'd ever been off work. Jordan had for months avoided that thought, and now she found it didn't freak her out as much as she thought it would. The world wouldn't stop—though her world was changing, irreversibly. And she was ready.

She could also understand why Ellie had been a tad defensive. It had to be strange for her to come to this scene, with Bethany, and Veronica. To Jordan, much of it was a reminder of a past she was proud to have overcome, and they all had emerged on this other side as friends, or, at times, adults who managed to be friendly.

However, she was interested in Bethany's answer as well.

"There's nothing nefarious going on. But I met him on occasion, and I found him a little...off. Could be just me."

"Yeah, it could be just you," Jordan agreed, earning her an indulgent smile from her ex.

Then again, it wasn't like she hadn't noticed Shriver's constant attempts at making friends and seeking her out especially.

But her latest interaction with him had been an exception. Someone else would solve that case, because Jordan was going to have a baby. Still no freaking out.

❦

Sam Potts opened the door to Ellie with a worried expression.

"She's still here?"

"Yes, but not for much longer, I'm afraid." Ellie followed her into the living room where Janine was pacing, coming to an abrupt halt.

"Hi, Janine. Would you mind tell me what's going on?"

"I spoke too soon, that's all. I'm not sure what I saw."

"Sit down, please."

Janine perched on the corner of a worn couch, and Ellie pulled herself a chair, sitting across from her.

"Talk to me, please. I promise you we're doing everything we can to keep you safe."

"I can't hide out here forever. I need to pay my rent."

"It won't be necessary to hide forever."

"Damn right. You can't make me testify in court, right?"

Ellie suppressed a sigh. She hadn't reached Esposito but left a message.

"It's true, nobody can force you. But the D.A. might think about charging you for lying to the authorities and wasting everyone's time. Detective Shriver might not be happy about false accusations." She was grasping at straws. To Ellie's surprise, Janine flinched at the mention of Shriver. "Did he or his lawyer try to talk to you?"

"Nobody talked to me. Nobody but Chad, that is. He needed me to come back to work, and I can't have this lady," she pointed at Sam, "hanging around. Or you. I'm really sorry."

"It's not that easy," Ellie said softly. "You identified him, by name, in front of several witnesses, including my lieutenant and his. That's not going to go away just like that."

"Maybe I don't care. Charge me. I don't want to end up like Alicia."

Ellie didn't want that either. She also had to resist the urge to shake Janine, though she was well aware that the woman was afraid and already used to everyone around her trying to intimidate her. Someone had succeeded.

"Did Chad threaten you? Do you think he knows more about Alicia's murder than he told us?"

"Hell if I know." She shook her head. "You can't use my testimony against the cop, that's all. I'll lose my job, and I'll be back out on the street. There's worse than Chad, and besides, everyone of his buddies will know it was me."

"Look, Janine. Remember Meg told you that you could trust me? I need you to trust me now. We can't help you if you don't talk to us."

"There's nothing to talk about. I need to leave. If you want to arrest me, do it already."

"I'd like you to come in tomorrow, no wait, we'll have breakfast first and then we meet with the A.D.A. She can give you an even clearer picture of your options."

"I think I know what my options are. Until you decide to lock me up, I need to work. Please."

Ellie understood that she was quickly running out of options. She went with what she hoped was an acceptable compromise. "Meet me tomorrow morning. I know for a fact you won't be working then."

"I guess I can do that."

"Thank you. Good night, Janine."

She gestured for Sam to follow her. Outside the apartment, she said, "I still want to know who's going in and out. Call me any time."

Sam chuckled. "I think you've realized I'm not above doing that."

"Good. Something will shake loose. Now I'll go home to my wife and hope that all food cravings can wait until tomorrow."

On second thought, she might ask Jordan to come to that breakfast, to everyone's benefit. Jordan had succeeded in getting one of her former informants, Darla Pierson, off the street, so perhaps she could give her some pointers. That, and their fridge was once again almost empty.

When Maria Doss arrived at the table, almost everyone was ready to go. Jordan offered to stay for one more drink, wine for her colleague, another iced tea for her.

"That's awesome," Maria commented. "Finally, someone could bring me up to date on everything that's going on around here. I get that Ellie is looking at Shriver, but what does the FBI have to do with it?"

"I'm not sure."

Truth be told, Jordan wondered if Bethany hung around for a bit just to stir up things, but she might harbor some residual paranoia about her. Bethany did whatever she felt like doing. If she was interested in a case, she would follow up, regardless of personal connections. Though having seen her reaction to Shriver, Jordan was intrigued. Maternal leave or not, she wouldn't be able to turn that off.

"I see. The gossip I was hoping for, I won't be getting it from you."

"Sorry about that. But I don't really know all that much. You're aware I've done more phone calls and paperwork in the past weeks than in all my years on the job."

"Yeah, I'm aware. So, you're all ready for the little one to arrive?"

"Loaded question. As ready as I'll ever be, I guess."

"You'll do great," Maria predicted.

"Thanks." Since her private life was an oftentimes subject of conversation these days, Jordan decided the question was only fair. "Did you and Valerie think about...?"

"God no. First of all, we are all in awe that you found the time in the first place, and besides, we'll be happy to be another couple of cool aunties who can go home once it's time to change diapers or deal with a tantrum."

"Charming," Jordan commented, amused.

"Yeah. You know your friends. Would you like to share a cab? I think your dad is giving me a stern look for keeping you up, and he's right."

"Sure, why not? I'm certain the stern look is for me though."

Maria made the call, and they went to wait outside, where the temperature had cooled notably.

"Are those snowflakes?" Jordan asked in disbelief.

"I guess so. Didn't you hear the forecast? They said there might be a storm. The last time this happened, Waters said it was proof that global warming is a hoax. Oh, how much I don't miss him."

"I won't argue with you on that."

It had taken a while, but Lieutenant Carroll had been serious about following up on accusations and cleaning house. Now Lieutenant Daniels would have to do the same.

She was curious about Ellie's efforts, and still slightly baffled about seeing her go to Derek first. She still wasn't used to that.

Chapter Fifteen

T he rest of the night had been fairly quiet, with a good night's sleep for both of them after Ellie had caught up Jordan on the latest developments. As she'd expected, Jordan agreed to come to breakfast the next day and talk to Janine.

That's where Ellie's optimism about how they might be able to move forward, took a hit, and it wasn't the only one. Icy streets made the commute longer than expected, but when they arrived at the diner ten minutes later than the scheduled time, Janine was nowhere to be seen. Her cell phone was turned off, but Valerie Esposito finally answered hers.

"Hey, Ellie, I'm sorry I didn't get back to you earlier, but I was swamped. Where are we on Janine?"

"I'm afraid nowhere. She wants to retract. I know she's afraid, though it's hard to tell who she's most afraid of. I would have liked all of us to sit down, but now she's AWOL. She was supposed to meet me this morning, so far, no luck. I'll have to make some calls."

"You do that. If you find her, you come here and I'll squeeze you in, but either way, keep me updated. We're giving Shriver an awful lot of time to get rid of anything compromising."

That was exactly what Ellie was afraid of. While the waitress refilled their coffees, she tried to reach Sam, but she was already off. Libby Marshall, the officer who had taken over, confirmed that the morning had passed without incident so far, though she hadn't seen Janine leave.

"I don't like it," Ellie said. "Wait for me?"

"I'll be here," Libby confirmed.

Ellie cast a regretful look at her plate. "I'm really sorry I'll have to leave you with this and the check."

Jordan didn't seem all too unhappy. "I'll live," she said. "Be careful?"

"Always. Love you. See you later."

Libby exited the unmarked car, and they walked across the street to Janine's apartment building.

"This might not be a perfect moment, but we realized we never gave you guys a baby shower," Libby remarked. "Jordan will be off work when, next week?"

"Yes, that's the plan. Wow, time did really fly by."

"It wouldn't be long, just a brunch maybe? I talked to Casey, and we felt really bad about it."

"That's good—wait, not you feeling bad. I mean, brunch would be great."

Ellie was grateful to know her friends cared, though it seemed strange to discuss her family in this context—strange, because she felt uncomfortable thinking of Janine who had so few options. They'd been lucky with Darla, and Meg and Ginny, but those successes too often felt like a drop in the ocean.

"Awesome. We can set a date later, then."

They walked along the hallway to Janine's door, both of them stopping cold when they realized the door was ajar.

Communicating without words, they slowly advanced on the door, and Libby pushed it open. No sound was coming from the apartment, and they quickly went inside the one-bedroom place with their guns drawn. Living area, bathroom and closet were empty. At this point, the silence felt oppressive as Ellie forced herself to walk into the bedroom, bracing herself. Janine lay on the floor, her eyes closed, a pool of blood still wet underneath her shoulder. Ellie dropped to her knees, hoping against all reason as she checked for a pulse.

"She's alive! Let's get an ambulance in here."

How was this possible? No one could have gone inside the apartment unseen, least of all Noah Shriver or Chad Warner—or could they?

Ellie cast a glance at Libby who had blanched.

"I didn't see anyone, I swear," she said.

"I believe you." Ellie had worked with Libby Marshall long enough to trust her. She had no answers. She stayed next to Janine's still form until the paramedics arrived and took her away, then she got up and walked to the window. It was closed, and besides, it would have taken Spiderman to climb up that wall. Had the perpetrator been hiding out in the building? Had they just missed him? The blood was just barely drying around the edges.

"It's a long shot, but he could still be in the building," Ellie said. She was already on the phone, calling for back-up. "Let's search it top to bottom. We also need to check for Shriver's and Warner's alibis."

Taking action made her feel better, but only slightly. She should have insisted on Janine telling them what she knew, have Sam stay with her.

Maybe she should have stayed.

⁓

Back at the station, Ellie called the hospital to learn that Janine was still hanging on by a thread. Then she went into the briefing room to meet with the lieutenant and Derek. Libby and Sam were also present.

"I know I should have handled this differently," Ellie began. "I messed up."

"She wanted to retract," Derek reminded her.

"We tried everything," Sam added. "She knew more than anyone what the dangers were."

"While I'm inclined to agree with Detective Harding here, this is the situation we now have to deal with," the lieutenant said. "Where are we on evidence? Alibis?"

"Lots of prints. The lab is still on that." Ellie was feeling light-headed, and it wasn't for the amount of blood she'd seen in the bedroom. What if the man who had murdered Alicia and tried to kill Janine as well, got away? What if they killed more people, and it was her fault? "There was a partial footprint. We'll be off to see Warner in a minute. We haven't reached Shriver yet, but his lawyer hinted at an alibi."

"Well, he'll have to do more than hint. Carpenter's still trying his phone?"

"Yes."

"All right. Unit's on its way to his apartment. Come back right here after you spoke to Warner."

"Yes, sir. Let's go," she said to Derek. Libby and Sam, looking worried, followed them out of the office, not before they'd all gotten a glimpse at Lieutenant Carroll's frustrated posture.

"He's right, you know," Ellie said as she and Derek walked to her car. "I should have done something."

"Like what? Shriver knows everyone's looking at him. If he did it, it was extremely stupid, especially since she wanted to retract. I know we have to check Warner off the list, but he had an interest in her being alive and working. Changing her testimony was probably his idea."

"People who kill others don't always follow reason."

"You got me there. Someone snapped—but then it might be about more than Janine's testimony. You couldn't see this coming, Ellie."

She wasn't in the mood to argue either way.

⁂

"Alicia and now Janine?" It was hard to tell if Warner's concerned expression was genuine, or for show. "God, I hate you guys. I thought you were looking at one of your own?"

No, Ellie thought, that didn't sound like he cared about the women at all.

"We are looking at every possible angle," Derek said. "Just humor us. Where were you this morning, between five a.m. and now?"

"In bed. There are two lovely ladies that can confirm that."

Despite the seriousness of the situation, Ellie barely refrained from rolling her eyes. "I'm sure they don't have much of a choice either way."

"Think what you want, but the girls that work for me are much better off than working the streets. I pay them, they make me a lot of money. Killing anyone isn't good for business."

As much as she disliked him, Ellie was tempted to believe he told the truth, and she sensed that Derek thought the same.

"What about the money Alicia received from her client, in order to get out? You took it from her, refused to give it back?"

"Alicia had no family, and I had access to that account all the time. I'm basically the heir, so why would I give it back to the guy? That was pathetic, by the way. He got played like a rookie on his first day. She was never going to leave me."

He got played—angry enough to kill her?

"You try that often, rip off clients with sums like that?" Derek wondered out loud.

"Hey, that was Alicia's idea, I didn't know until she told me about the money. She asked me for advice where to put it."

That was probably stretching to truth.

"Right."

"Hey, what do you know, she had skills, and that guy obviously appreciated them. What can I say? I'm sad she's dead, and I hope Janine will be well enough to come back to work soon. As for this guy…poor sucker."

"Janine said you wanted her to retract her testimony? Why? If it helped draw attention away from you?"

Warner laughed. "Come on, how many times do I have to say this? I didn't do anything. With or without Janine, Shriver was going down, and I needed to run my place without having the police show up all the time—like you are now. I wanted her to wrap it up and do her job, that's all. Maybe she misunderstood something."

"Fair enough," Ellie said. "Just tell me what that stain on your shoe is."

❧

Meri was unusually antsy, and perhaps she was as eager to come into the world as Jordan was for her to do just that. She was neither here nor there, at work, but increasingly out of the loop when things happened fast, and she wasn't taking part in the action. It made her feel like an imposter. She couldn't wait for this phase to end, to have time off, for the event she tended to skip in her mind, and the life after, with a new baby.

It was strange to think of this now as everyone was busy with the rapidly developing case.

Warner had a good story, but if it was Janine's blood on his shoes, he was in a predicament. That didn't mean Shriver was out of the woods. She had tried his phone many times, leaving a couple of messages that stressed how urgent it was that they'd talk to him. So far, no response. She sat with another tea, thinking about that expensive chocolate basket and his flimsy explanations.

Meri, I hope you'll never get this good at attracting psychopaths. Jordan hoped that this wasn't where biology came in, because Kathryn didn't have that great a track record.

Spooked, she dialed the number another time, and to her surprise, the phone was answered.

"Hey, Noah, is that you? Jordan here. This is urgent. You need to come in."

There was a long pause, and she almost gave up on a response, when he said, "Don't worry. My lawyer's handling this. I just wanted to say goodbye."

"Come on. This is not how this works, and you know it."

"Don't bother tracking the phone. You're not going to find me."

"Don't do this. You can still turn this around. Warner was arrested this morning. I know you only wanted to help Alicia."

"I know you understand that, but no one else does. Thank you, Jordan. I won't forget it."

"We can talk about this. You come in now, we can clear up everything."

"I appreciate you trying, but it's far too late for that. I'm sorry."

Jordan flinched, but she didn't hear the sound she'd feared. He had ended the call. When she called again, a robotic voice told her that the number was no longer in service. Damn it.

She got to her feet, then clutched the edge of her desk the next moment. The painful stab was gone after a few deep breaths, but its intensity surprised and worried her.

"No way, little one," she whispered. "When I said 'soon,' I meant we're going to have another quiet couple of weeks.

Right?" When she could stand straight again, she went to Carroll's office and knocked to update him on the call.

~

Warner's attorney came to meet them at the department. She was young, and female. *Figures*, Ellie thought, already tired. She had called the hospital again and found out that the doctors that treated Janine were cautiously optimistic.

"It's very obvious to me why my client is here."

"Because a woman he threatened was viciously attacked, and he had blood on his shoes?" A.D.A. Esposito asked sarcastically. "We'll soon have confirmation that it was hers."

"I wouldn't be so sure. First of all, he says he didn't threaten her, just asked her to come back to work. But I get it. He looks great as a suspect, right? A man who hasn't done much to follow the straight and narrow. Mr. Warner isn't very likeable, is he?" Warner snorted. His attorney continued, unfazed. "He runs a strip club. He looked the other way when his girlfriend slept with other men for money. But does that make him a murderer?"

"Counselor, aren't you missing the point here?"

"My point is you have a suspect, someone who was already suspected in the murder of Mr. Warner's girlfriend, for a good reason. As far as I know, Detective Shriver has come up with a thin alibi via his lawyer but refuses to come in to tell his side of the story." She shrugged. "It's not like I don't understand. He's a cop. His career is on the line, and so much more, and all of it could come back to the department. I get it. He's a terrible suspect. Mr. Warner looks so much better."

"Are you trying to say someone in this room is trying to cover for Shriver?" Derek asked incredulously. "You better be careful with that."

While Ellie agreed with him, she had to admit it wasn't a bad strategy for the attorney and her client. After the Waters scandal, she would like to believe the owner of a strip club rather than a detective was responsible for a murder and an attempted murder. Like Derek had told her earlier, Warner didn't have much of a reason for wanting to kill Janine—but it would be hard to argue if that blood on his shoes turned out to be hers.

"I'm not accusing anyone," the lawyer defended herself. "This is just the context I think we should all be aware of."

"What about you, Mr. Warner?" Ellie asked. "Can you tell us how the blood ended up on your shoes? If you were in Janine's apartment at any time after the attack, we need to know now."

He exchanged a look with his attorney, and she nodded.

"I have no freaking idea how it happened," he said. "I told you the truth. I got up this morning and put on my clothes, and shoes. I didn't have a lot of time, so I didn't see the blood. I can't tell you how it got there."

"When is the last time you saw Detective Shriver?"

"A few weeks ago, when he last came to the club. I didn't speak to him."

He stuck to his testimony, hadn't changed a bit of it since they had first sought him out. Meanwhile, Shriver was in hiding. What did that mean? Why wasn't he coming in if he was innocent?

"We're done here. You have nothing to hold Mr. Warner," the attorney said. "He has a business, regardless of whether we approve of its nature, and strong ties to the community."

The latter was more than stretching it, but she was right that they couldn't do much else at the moment. Too many loose ends, it was giving her a headache. At least, Jordan would be off work coming next week. At least, that was progress.

"Don't leave town," Ellie said.

Chapter Sixteen

B y the time Jordan cleaned up her desk on Friday evening, Shriver was still hiding out, and he hadn't tried to contact her again. She needed to shift her thoughts from the possibilities to the near future, and perhaps she was freaking out a little now, because there was nothing to distract her, not anymore. So many people had assured her she'd be a good mother, and for the longest time, Jordan had told herself there was no way she could do worse than the circumstances she'd grown up with.

Time to put up, prove herself.

Well, almost.

"You're ready to go home?" she asked Ellie who had appeared in front of her desk.

"I'm sorry, no, this is all taking longer than I expected. Do you need a ride home?"

"Why? No. I could drive yesterday, so I'm pretty sure I can do it today." Briefly, she thought about that instant of pain earlier, and decided it was nothing to worry about. Little hints, but definitely not the real thing.

"You'll be okay with Kathryn?"

They had invited her to dinner, not anticipating how the case would go. At this point, though, Jordan didn't think she had anything left to prove, and fortunately, Kathryn had mostly understood that.

"Don't worry. It'll be fine."

"Okay then." Ellie leaned in for a quick kiss. "Be careful. It's been freezing again."

"Really. I know how to drive in the winter." Jordan kissed her back to make sure her words didn't sound like sniping too much. "Good luck."

Ellie sighed. "Thanks. I can use it."

⁂

Banter aside, the roads actually weren't pleasant to drive, so when Jordan made it home, she didn't have time to do anything but lay out some take-out menus before Kathryn rang the doorbell.

After a hesitant hug, she came inside.

"Hey. I'm glad you could make it." They had made big strides to improve their relationship, difficult work for both of them—that didn't mean there wouldn't be awkward moments. "Ellie's still at work, but she said we shouldn't wait for her. Can I offer you something to drink?"

"I'll have water, but I can get it."

"Come on. I worked until today. I still have a few weeks." Closer to a couple, but that was a fact that came with mixed emotions. Kathryn followed her into the kitchen where Jordan poured a glass of water for each of them.

"You could help me set the table though." She hadn't missed Kathryn's gaze go to the ultrasound pictures pinned to the fridge.

"Yeah, that time went by real quick."

A long pause followed, making it hard to deny how many potential minefields any conversation about pregnancy and motherhood held for them.

"So quick," Kathryn said wistfully. "But you don't have to worry about anything. Your baby is healthy, and you have a lot of support."

And having no support at all was terrible. It was not an excuse for everything that had followed. Those were just facts she had come to acknowledge, and she'd been able to take the emotion out of it. For the most part.

"I do."

"And look at those maternity clothes. I'm not sure anything nice like that even existed in my time." The fact that she mentioned it only now, showed how much Kathryn had kept her distance in the past months.

"A friend of Ellie's works in a boutique. They have a good selection. Let's go set that table now."

"Wait a second. I wanted to wait until Ellie's here, but I hope she won't mind. I'd like to give you something."

"You didn't have to." Kathryn had turned her life around in many ways, and Jordan had even come to a point where she found her believable. However, she was aware Kathryn didn't have a lot of financial freedom.

"I did. This is my grandchild too." As if to escape any argument on the subject matter, she went back to the living room where she picked up a bag she'd brought with her.

"Open it, please."

Inside the bag was a wrapped box, containing a tiny romper, hat and socks.

"I know it's not much, but it never hurts to have some to spare."

"It's perfect. Thank you."

When she embraced Kathryn, hormones finally got the better of her. Jordan was truly grateful for the place they had come to, even though she couldn't help hoping her own daughter would never have equally conflicted emotions about her.

"No sign of Shriver. We're still waiting on lab results... Oh, and you better get ready for this. Folks at work want to throw a baby shower," Ellie told her later that night. Kathryn had left a while ago, and they were sharing the re-heated leftovers of the meal Jordan had ordered.

She was feeling better now, if completely exhausted. The last few days had been draining—she'd mustered as much energy as possible for the last work hours, but now she felt like sleeping all the way until the baby arrived.

"As long as they bring everything they want to eat or drink, I'm fine, but isn't it a little late? We have everything we need to get started."

"Yes, but everyone's been so busy, and they want to celebrate. But it's up to you."

"Like I said, I'm good as long as I don't need to do anything. I plan to be lazy until the day."

"Yeah. You'll do great."

There was nothing but confidence and reassurance in Ellie's voice, and Ellie of all people should know. Jordan had just one small correction to make.

"*We*'ll do great."

Saturday morning, Ellie stole out of bed while Jordan was fast asleep. She was going to meet Derek at the hospital where Janine was finally out of the woods and well enough, considering, to talk to investigators. The doctor had already warned her on the phone that she didn't have much to say.

While Ellie would have liked to stay next to her wife in the warm bed, part of her still got excited knowing she was part of that team she'd always wanted to belong to. Even if that meant shivering in a hospital parking garage at seven a.m.

Derek pulled up in the spot next to hers five minutes later.

"Damn, it's cold," he said, pulling up the collar of his coat. "More proof this planet is going to hell."

"Cheerful. I don't disagree, but I'd like to see my baby before that happens."

"Don't worry. I think they said we got ten more years of crappy weather before it all ends. All right. Let's see what Janine can tell us."

In the hospital room, Janine looked almost as white as the pillow she was leaning against, dark circles under her eyes.

"I'll leave you to it, but don't overstay your welcome, detectives," the nurse warned. "She's been through a lot and needs her rest."

When they stepped closer to the bed, Janine gave them a faint smile.

"This is what...happens when you don't listen...to the police? So stupid."

"You did what you thought was right for you." Ellie wasn't going to double down when the woman was already beating herself up over her actions. "However, it is important that you help us protect you. Did you see the person that shot you?"

Janine shook her head. "No. He wore...a mask." Her cough fortunately passed and didn't set off one of the machines she was hooked to.

Ellie made an effort not to show her disappointment. "Do you remember anything else about him? Was he familiar?"

"What do you mean?"

"Could it be Chad?"

"No way," she said with surprising vehemence.

Ellie exchanged a look with Derek who shrugged.

"Why do you say that?"

"He called me earlier that morning, said he'd expect me back at work, and congratulated me, because I took back my statement. He was at the club, I could hear people in the background. Why would he want to kill me?"

Why indeed?

"Thank you, Janine. If you can think of anything else, please let us know."

Ellie needed caffeine badly, and she didn't have to convince Derek to stop at a coffee shop on their way back. With a black coffee and a chocolate chip muffin in front of her, she was ready to sort out her thoughts.

"Warner had motive. With a little luck, we'll be able to place him in that apartment—his shoes anyway, and the only person who might have an interest in setting him up, likely didn't have the opportunity. If Warner was there, but didn't kill her? That brings us back to Shriver. And we can't ask him because he refuses to come in."

"Lawyer says he was with him during the time of the attack but doesn't know where he is now." Derek sighed. "All extremely convenient—for everyone except us. No matter how we put it together, there are some pieces that don't fit."

"I hope Shriver will turn up. He was awfully obvious the whole time, going to the club, paying Alicia Fox...I hate to say Warner's lawyer had a point. I'd prefer him as a subject rather than another cop, but we have to go where the evidence leads us."

"Well, at the moment, it still leads us to Warner. We'll have to check those phone records. Under the circumstances, I'm sure we can move quickly on those, and Shriver. He's got issues, no doubt about it. But perhaps we're lucky and Daniels doesn't get even worse headlines than we had with Waters."

"Yeah. Let's see what we can do about those records. I'd like to see if he was really in the club when he called Janine."

Their snack finished, they left the coffee shop to head back to the station. Ellie wondered briefly if Jordan had gotten up yet.

***

In his mind, they all started to blend together, attraction, hope, and inevitable failure. Was he making the wrong choices, taking the wrong actions? No, he thought to himself. It was all their fault, her fault, being so stubborn and unwilling to see reality. What else could he have done? What could he do to make them see? The story had to end, one way or another. He was always supposed to come out the hero, but now it would be so much harder.

The woman next to him gave him a knowing smile when he picked up the item. He found her demeanor a little too flirty, given the context.

"First time dad?" she asked, perhaps referring to the fact that he'd stood in front of the bin with the soft toys for newborn babies a little too long. He relaxed his fingers around the soft plush fabric and forced a smile in return.

"Something like that," he said. "I'll take this one."

Chapter Seventeen

Trying to piece together Warner's actions at the time of the attempted murder and shortly before, proved puzzling: He had made a call to Janine's number as she'd said, and the signal put his phone in the vicinity of the strip club. If he knew those records could help his story, why didn't he or the lawyer mention it? Why not mention at all that he had called Janine?

There was another theory, that someone else had used his cell phone to help him create an alibi—no. Ellie shook her head to herself.

Janine would have known if it wasn't him? She was still weak but had been pretty clear on what she did and didn't remember.

"I think I have an idea why he didn't want to mention it," the tech said. "Look at where the next call puts him?"

Ellie took a look at the map, understanding right away. "Wow. He called her, and the next time he uses his phone, he's right there on her corner? No wonder he didn't want us to know. Can we find out who he called?"

"I need a little more time for that, but yes."

"Great. Let us know as soon as you're done," Derek said. "Now we're getting somewhere."

He'd barely finished his sentence when Ellie's phone rang. The lab tech on the other end confirmed that the blood on Warner's shoes belonged to Janine.

⁂

"It's the weekend, damn it. Can't you give it a rest for a few hours?" Warner muttered when they showed up at his front door.

"We might if you had told us the truth the first time," Ellie said.

"What the hell are you talking about?"

"Who did you call after getting your shoes dirty in Janine's apartment? Your phone records tell a pretty interesting story about your whereabouts that day. And that blood was Janine's."

He shrugged. "Couldn't help you there. Various people use that phone."

"What people?"

"People that work for me. You met my bouncer...and my lawyer. Both of them have used it, and I don't always ask where they were at the time."

"They borrow your shoes as well?" Ellie asked incredulously.

Derek's expression revealed his irritation. "All right, Mr. Warner." he said. "Please turn around. You're under arrest for the attempted murder of Janine Kepler. You have the right to remain silent. Anything you say—"

"Okay, okay! Wait!" Warner interrupted him. "I probably shouldn't talk to you without my lawyer, but all right, here it is. I called Janine, because I wanted to see her and talk about the future. The door was open, and I stepped inside and saw her...I thought she was dead. That's all. I didn't do it."

Ellie had a hard time keeping her expression neutral. If he told the truth, it meant he didn't even care to check if Janine was alive. She was sick and tired of people like him, who didn't see anything in women but the money they could make them. In the past few years, she'd been confronted with too many like him.

"What did you do?" she asked.

"I called my brother Jay, and we decided we'd lay low. If I'd managed to change my shoes in the meantime, you'd have never known..."

"That you left her to die? You're not going to get out of this so easily," she said, not bothering to hide her anger.

"I told you, I thought she was dead!"

"But you didn't check, didn't care to call 911."

He shrugged, doing nothing to disavow her of the notion that alive or dead, he didn't care about the women. At least the club would likely be shut down. Small victories, she reminded herself.

"While you were in the building, did you see anyone else?" Derek asked.

"I wish I could help you, but no. I got out as quickly as possible, didn't see anyone."

"All right. That changes things slightly."

"I'm not under arrest?" he asked, sounding hopeful.

"Oh, you are," Derek informed him while Ellie called in the uniformed officers that had accompanied them. "You failed to report a crime. You didn't call 911. There's a whole host of things we need to sort out. You can call your lawyer from the station."

"This is bullshit," Warner muttered. He remained silent after that, though, and didn't protest when the officers led him out of the apartment. Ellie and Derek left, too.

"This also complicates things," Ellie remarked.

"No kidding," he agreed.

Jordan had spent a lazy morning which was both pleasant and slightly odd. She didn't spend every single day thinking about work—but in the recent past, whenever she'd taken a break, it was always with Ellie. Ellie, however, was at work, trying to solve the mystery surrounding Noah Shriver and Alicia Fox's death.

She hadn't been able to think happy thoughts all the time during her pregnancy, but if anything, they'd make sure that Meri would be prepared for a world that wasn't always kind.

After receiving a text from Ellie telling her she wasn't going to be home for lunch, Jordan called Pauline to see what plans she and Jack had, and they offered to come get her.

Noah Shriver had vanished without a trace. His lawyer had told them everything he could, and he seemed believable.

The Velvet Rope remained closed, its owner in custody and currently discussing future steps with his lawyer.

Ellie was about to call it a day and meet Jordan at her parents' house, when Derek's phone rang. He made gestures for her to wait, and after he'd ended the call, he said,

"Weekend's not starting yet. Shriver's ex-wife has returned, and she's willing to talk to us."

"Okay. That's good news."

"Let's hope so.

Ashley Stratton, formerly Shriver, lived in a two-story house in a suburban neighborhood, the house she'd shared with her now ex-husband.

"Homicide? This has got to be serious. Did something happen to him?"

"That's what we're trying to find out," Ellie said diplomatically. "When did you last talk?"

She scrunched up her face in thought. "Honestly? I can't tell you. Sometime last year maybe, there were some papers we needed to sign. Divorce comes with a flood of paperwork."

Ellie shared a silent look with Derek, seeing her own sentiments reflected. They never wanted to find out.

"It's important that we find him. Can you think of any place, any property of his?"

"I'm really sorry. This was, for both of us, the first place we bought. We shared a smaller apartment downtown before. Noah wasn't keen on spending big sums."

This was the same man who had paid 15K to a woman twice—to help her? Or because they'd already been blackmailing him? With what? She was afraid they were going to hit a dead end again.

"Whatever it is you're after, I hope you can help him," Ashley said. "He wouldn't talk to me, ever, about the job or..." She laughed bitterly. "Anything else, really. That's not a marriage, is it? I mean, who can live like this? But there was something troubling him, and whatever it is, I hope he'll figure it out."

The subject wasn't an easy one approach.

"Ms. Stratton, I know this is difficult, and I'm sorry, but we have to ask you this. Was he ever violent to you?"

"You mean, did he hit me? Never." A long pause followed, her cheeks reddening. "No. You're not thinking...There was none of that stuff in the bedroom."

If Noah Shriver wasn't guilty of anything, why was he running? The picture forming in Ellie's mind was becoming clearer bit by bit. Shriver had presented a much different image to the women he encountered in his job than to his former wife.

"Is he religious?"

"That's quite the departure from your previous question." Ashley gave a nervous laugh. "I'm not sure what to say to that. We went to church on a fairly regular basis, but with his job, it wasn't always possible. He's no zealot, if that's what you wanted to know. An old-fashioned gentleman, maybe, and I did find that attractive...the lack of communication, not so much."

"Thank you, Ms. Stratton. If you can think of anything else, especially regarding where he might be, or if he contacts you, please call right away."

She took the card Ellie handed her. "I'll do that."

❦

"Do you believe her?" Derek asked when they were back in the car.

"She cares about him. That doesn't mean she's lying."

"It doesn't have to mean she's not."

"True. I guess we won't know anything more until Monday."

"Yeah, I'll see you then. Next Friday is okay for the baby shower? Kate can't wait."

Ellie laughed. "You guys are cutting it close, but I think it will be fine." More serious, she added, "Let's hope we can close this case before."

"That's the idea."

❦

After dinner at Jack and Pauline's, Ellie and Jordan spent a quiet weekend planning the future.

"So, about that baby shower…" Jordan began, "I suppose it's the last big event…"

"Before the big event." Ellie shook her head in wonder. "It's not long now."

"No. I can't tell you how grateful I am."

"Is there anything you think we should do, before?" Ellie wondered. "Would you have liked a photo shoot?"

"Hell no," Jordan protested, laughing. "I think you've taken enough pictures from every possible angle. I wouldn't mind if you wanted to do one once Meri is ready. And the day I fit into my uniform again—or the wedding dress. Or any regular clothes, really."

It was a rare moment for them to be completely focused on themselves, Ellie reflected, no work or family, or friends sharing. She enjoyed it. She also knew it wouldn't last forever. For the time being, it was an amazing, new experience. And in about two weeks from now, they'd be three.

Chapter Eighteen

The reprieve lasted until Monday morning, when the judge decided Chad Warner didn't present a flight risk. Jordan had joined Ellie in court, and she went with her into Valerie's office afterwards, quietly following the conversation.

"What the hell!" Valerie slammed a folder onto her desk. "What makes him think Warner wouldn't take the money he extorted from a cop and flee the country?"

"Such good ties to the community?" Ellie suggested sarcastically.

"I didn't see this coming at all. I must be losing my touch."

"No, no one could see this coming," Jordan felt obliged to say. "But honestly, why would he run? He has his story straight now, doesn't he? And he maintains he's innocent—nothing looks guiltier than jumping bail."

"Unless he has other things to hide. I don't know." Valerie sighed. "Why are you even here?"

"Emotional support? So far it seems like it's not doing much."

"Yes, that's funny. I need to go back to work. Good luck you two with everything." She made an all-encompassing gesture. "Baby's almost due?"

"Two weeks."

"Yeah, well, that doesn't have to mean much. My cousin went for brunch with her friends, because she still had three weeks, and her water broke right after her first Virgin Mimosa."

This wasn't anything Jordan wanted to hear at the moment, especially given where they were.

"A Virgin Mimosa is orange juice."

"Not my point," Valerie returned, laughing, "but you know what I mean. Not all babies stick to the schedule."

"I think we're fine. Ellie needs to go back to work too. Let's go?"

She turned to Ellie who looked concerned all of a sudden.

"Something happens and I'm not there, you call 911, right?"

"Nothing's going to happen while you're not there. Come on."

⁓

Kate stopping by to take Ellie out for lunch was a highlight in an otherwise dreary day—no news on Shriver yet. At least Chad Warner seemed to be aware of the enormous chance he'd been given, probably doing what he could to preserve what was left of his business.

"You must be so excited," Kate said as they sat down.

She'd been so far, but now all Ellie could think about was Valerie's cousin having her baby early. These things happened. Stress was probably a factor...but Jordan was okay, right? In fact, Ellie had rarely seen her as calm and centered as in recent weeks. The doctor had assured them that everything was fine with mother and baby. Nothing would happen that wasn't supposed to.

"I am," she said, with a little delay. "It's really a miracle to us."

"You think you'll want to have a baby too?"

"Whoa, slow down, let's welcome this one first?"

Kate, of course, had lived through some tough experiences, and she didn't waste a lot of time when going for the tougher questions. That, and she and Ellie had been friends for many years now.

"Sure. I'm just curious."

Ellie gave the question some thought. "Actually, I don't know, and that's not the answer I would have given you a year ago. Jordan has been so great, and we both really want a family. But I think if it's us and Meri, I'll be good. We'll be good."

Kate nodded. "I can see that. You have been so good at making the right, mature decisions." She laughed a little. "I think it's been rubbing off on me."

"You are thinking about…"

"No. But I saw Jensen's mom this weekend."

"How did that go?"

"She's the most amazing woman," Kate said. "She's still grieving, of course, and in a way, we both are. But I am also happy."

"I'm happy for you, then."

Ellie thought they both might have to renew their make-up in the restroom, but there was no time. Her phone rang, putting an end to her musings.

"Speak of the…It's your husband. I think that means my lunch break is cut short."

"Don't worry, I'll get the check," Kate offered as Ellie answered the call.

"Hey, what's up?"

"I got a call from Ms. Stratton. Shriver sent her a cryptic text message. We're trying to trace it, no luck so far."

"I'll be right there. You're at the precinct?"

"I'm still at her house. Meet me there?"

"Sure. I'll be there in twenty."

When Ellie left the restaurant, it occurred to her that Kate's reaction was very different from Jordan's in a situation like this. While Jordan couldn't wait to get back, Kate seemed comfortable with the doors she'd closed.

It was all about choices.

She wondered if they were about to find out which choices Noah Shriver had made.

❧

Ashley Stratton looked pale and frazzled, and the moment Ellie got to read the message she'd received from her ex-husband, she understood why.

It read like a suicide note.

I hope you can forgive me someday, but it's the only way I can find peace.

"I don't understand this. For months, nothing, and then this? What does it mean? What the hell has he gotten himself into?"

"That's what we're trying to figure out," Derek reminded her calmly.

"Well, figure it out faster! He might hurt himself."

Ellie caught Derek's glance. Perhaps he was thinking the same thing she was—himself or others. He might have already done whatever he'd been alluding to in that message.

"We'll do whatever we can to find him. I'll have an officer stay here with you in case he texts again, or calls."

"Thank you. "Ashley had already answered her ex-husband's text.

Where are you? Let's talk. I'll be here.

The answer came right away.

I can't.

174

Acting on instinct, Ellie took Derek aside. "Look, I don't want to be paranoid, but you know the story, and you saw that giant chocolate basket. I'd like to check in on Jordan right now."

He nodded.

"You do that, I'll wrap up here."

Ellie took out her cell phone and called Jordan's number, suppressing a relieved sigh when Jordan picked up after the second ring.

"Hey. You miss me already?"

"I do, but that's not why I'm calling. Shriver has been sending cryptic messages to his ex-wife. I just wanted to make sure everything is all right."

"I'm fine," Jordan said. "I understand your concern, but I'll keep the door locked and the phone near. I don't think he's going to contact me anymore."

"Better be safe than sorry, right?"

"Yeah. Be careful. I'll see you later."

Seconds after she ended the call, her phone rang again, the caller ID showing Maria Doss this time.

"I'm at the *Velvet Rope*," Maria said without preamble. "Guess who was strangled with an actual rope?"

"Oh, fuck." Ellie had no doubt as to who had murdered Warner, feeling a bit guilty but relieved that Shriver would have no time to seek out Jordan now.

She shook her head at what looked like truly twisted reasoning. She could understand frustration and anger toward someone like Warner, but even an interpretation of vigilante justice didn't hold when Shriver had likely killed one of the women he claimed to protect.

"Yeah, my thoughts exactly. Where are you and Derek now?"

"Still at Ms. Stratton's. I can come over. I guess Derek's going back to the precinct to see where we are on those cell phone records. See you in a bit."

A uniformed officer stayed behind at Stratton's residence after Ellie updated her temporary partner on the latest developments, and they parted ways.

❦

The killer had strangled Alicia Fox with his bare hands. The rope was still around Chad Warner's neck, but even so, the similarities were obvious and uncanny.

"It seems like through all of this, he didn't try very hard to cover up his tracks," Maria remarked. "Damn. Not our precinct this time, but it's going to be the kind of headline Carroll hates."

"Yeah. He worked some cases with us. IA isn't likely going to ignore that either."

"His brother, the bouncer, over there found him." She pointed to the man standing in the corner. "Warner went to work in the office this morning, brother came by to bring coffee and a snack, found him here."

"Rigor mortis has set in," Dr. Adams added. "I'll give you a more detailed idea of the timeline once I've had him on my table."

Ellie couldn't help thinking that this wasn't the priority right now.

"Let's put out a BOLO on Shriver," she said to Maria. They needed to find him. She worried that with every passing minute, it became less likely they'd find him alive.

❦

When the call came in, Jordan almost expected Noah Shriver to be on the other end of it, but instead it was Kathryn calling to ask how she was.

"I'm fine, thank you."

"Not long now. I'm so happy for you that you are able to enjoy every moment of it." She sounded wistful, and Jordan thought it was remarkable that she could make the most innocent remarks without realizing how much they stung. She didn't need to hear that Kathryn had likely hated every moment of her pregnancy, that she had no idea how to raise a child. But she had learned to handle Kathryn's particular brand of self-reproach, and to take herself out of the equation in the present.

"Thanks. I'm not sure about every moment, but yes, it's been kind of amazing." Maybe hearing that was just as hurtful to Kathryn even though she didn't mean it. "Listen, our friends are organizing a baby shower for this weekend, would you like to come? You don't have to bring anything, and besides, you gave me a gift already." Being clear and precise with each other mattered.

"I'd love to. Is there anything you need?"

"I'm good, but I think Ellie is looking for a photographer. But not until after the baby is born."

She didn't expect the enthusiastic answer from Kathryn. "Really? I know someone you might want to meet. She was homeless for a long time, but then fortunately got a chance, and she went back to school, a real talent. I can show you some of her work whenever you're ready."

"That sounds great. Sometime this week, maybe?"

"How's tonight?" Kathryn asked, hope in her voice.

Jordan didn't have much of an excuse, and besides, it couldn't harm to be prepared for anything, right? She'd be happy to take a look at the photographer's work. She knew that Kathryn had helped a few young women, after cleaning up her own life.

"Sure, why don't you come by for dinner? We can talk about it then. Ellie should be home."

"Do you mind if I bring Jim?"

Truth be told, Jordan's relationship, if anyone could call it that, with Kathryn's husband was a lot less complicated than the one she had with her biological mother. He hadn't cared much and had proven to be an equally neglectful parent back then. Jordan also didn't consider him her father in any sense. She imagined she could do one evening if it mattered to Kathryn.

"No, bring him, it's fine. We'll see you at six?"

"Yes, thank you. Should we bring anything?"

"No, we'll probably order...Excuse me for a moment," Jordan said when the buzzing sound announced a text message. Taking a look, she added, "I need to go. See you later."

Her next call went to Ellie's voicemail, and she tried Derek next.

"I can't reach Ellie," she said. "You will want to see this. I'm sending you a screenshot now."

"Ellie's probably still at the crime scene. Warner was found strangled earlier. Hold on, I'm getting your message." After a few seconds, he added, "Okay, I'm coming over."

"You really think that's necessary?" she asked, frowning. This wasn't the kind of drama she wanted to invite days before giving birth. Jordan silently cursed Shriver for not giving her much of a choice in the matter.

"Until I know, I prefer to make sure we don't get any bad surprises, especially now. Don't answer the door unless it's me."

"No argument for me. All right. Get here and we see about what to do next." *Damn it, Shriver, don't screw up my maternity leave.* Jordan took a deep breath and willed herself to calm. "We are calm," she told herself and Meri after Derek had ended the call. "For another couple of weeks, right?"

As if on cue, the pain hit her out of nowhere. Jordan waited for a few moments, trying to breathe through it, leaning back against the couch with a sigh. Not yet. It wasn't time. This didn't mean anything.

Right, Meri? You'll stay right where you are until after the shower—and Shriver is behind bars.

Chapter Nineteen

E llie didn't have any time to check her phone. Shriver had been caught on the security camera of a gas station, filling up his tank.

"He might try to get out of town," Maria Doss remarked as they headed to Ellie's car.

"He's going to feel cornered. Let's hope we catch him in a not so crowded area."

"Yeah. He was there a few minutes ago, so he must be on the highway, I assume. We are setting up roadblocks, and every available unit is in the area. He can't get out of this."

Uncomfortable with the thought, Ellie wondered how aware Shriver was of his reality—and how he'd react knowing he was caught. They had barely left the area where *The Velvet Rope* was located when the message came over the scanner:

Officers Marshall and Martin had spotted the suspect and were following him.

"I guess he's about to find out," Ellie said.

Thank you for listening. I hope someday soon, I'll have a chance to explain how much you mean to me. If it doesn't happen—know that I appreciate what you did for me.

"That sounds like he might want to stick close to you, and that's what's worrisome," Derek summed up the situation.

Jordan groaned. "I don't know where he got that idea. I didn't do anything for him. Nothing to warrant this kind of response anyway. This could mean anything. He might run, he might kill himself, he might be standing in my living room within the next hour."

"Well, the last one isn't going to happen. I'll check in with Ellie and Maria. As long as he stays in town, it will be easier to find him, and we'll keep an eye on your house."

She made no effort to hold back the curse. "Can I for once live in a house that's not haunted?"

"It's not haunted yet. And it was fun while it lasted when Kate and Ellie were living together."

"Hm. Yes. I think you can go back to the station, try to trace his cell. Let me know what you find?"

Derek, already on the phone, shook his head. "I'm staying here until we know something."

"You don't have to—"

He had turned away for a moment when the pain hit again. All the books and websites and doctor's advice hadn't prepared her for the reality that came with a sense of urgency.

"Are you okay? Wow. Jordan."

"Yes," she gasped. "Fine."

"I'm not so sure. How about I drive you to the hospital, just to be on the safe side? Ellie can join you later."

"No, that's not necessary. Kathryn and Jim are coming over for dinner. It's too early anyway..." This time, the curse had nothing to do with Shriver. "No, no, no." If she said it often enough, she might keep the pain, and what it meant, at bay for a little while longer.

"You're not convincing me. We're going to the hospital," he declared.

Jordan hated that she had to agree with him. "It's too early and I need Ellie to be here...but I really don't want to have my baby in the living room."

"That's the spirit. Let's go." At the front door, Derek helped her into her coat, surprisingly unfazed by the situation. "Don't worry. Didn't I tell you the story? When I was a rookie, a few weeks in uniform, I delivered a baby in a car when the couple was stuck in traffic."

"No, I never heard the story. I don't want to hear it now."

"Don't worry. Everything's going to be fine."

"Easy for you to say," she mumbled. This wasn't the way it was supposed to go. She hadn't exaggerated when she said she needed Ellie. At this moment, Jordan was terrified.

⌘

There was no way out. When Ellie and Maria arrived on the scene, one lane was closed. A couple of squad cars made sure Shriver was boxed in, his vehicle standing close to the guardrail.

Libby Marshall met them at the squad car.

"We asked him nicely to come out, no reaction so far."

"Well, let's ask him again," Ellie said. "I know he has a thing for Jordan, and I don't like it. I'm the closest he'll get to her, so maybe he'll go for that."

She had an uncanny feeling that this might not end as well as they all hoped. Shriver had to know that there was no way he could talk himself out of this mess. She had to try anyway.

Staying at a safe distance, she called his number. To Ellie's surprise, he picked up.

"Hi, Noah, it's Ellie."

"What do you want?" He laughed bitterly. "Well, whatever it is, it's too late for that."

"It doesn't have to be. Look, you know how it goes. You can make this a lot better by turning yourself in and cooperating."

"Better for whom? I'm done. That's what I know."

Ellie gritted her teeth before she said, "You care about Jordan, right?"

"What does that have to do with anything? I cared about a lot of people and look where that got me."

"She cares about you too. And I'm one hundred percent sure she doesn't want you to do anything stupid."

"We could say the same for you, couldn't we, Ellie? Don't come closer. I'm warning you."

"You'll do what?"

"Believe me, you don't want to find out."

"Come on. We can help you, but you have to help us a little bit."

"I've heard those lines before. Hell, I've said them many times. Believe me, there's no way anyone can help me."

"Why Chad Warner?" As Ellie kept talking, members of the tactical unit were advancing on the vehicle. "Why Alicia? One or the other, I can understand, but why both of them?"

"You are asking smart questions, I have to give you that. Two sides of the same coin, if you figure out what that means."

"I think I can, but why don't we find a way so you can really make your point clear. We talked to Ashley. I understand that a lot of things didn't turn out the way you hoped, and then Alicia and Chad took you for a ride. Obviously, you didn't make the best choices, and I think you know that, but we can understand you wanted to get back at them…"

"I'm so glad you understand, Ellie. That makes me feel a lot better."

The door on the driver's side opened, and the members of the tactical team halted.

"You're coming out now?"

"Yes, I'm coming out. I'm leaving my gun in the car."

"That's good. Thank you."

"Oh, you're welcome, Detective."

Something wasn't right, Ellie thought, even when he climbed out of the vehicle with his hands up. She hadn't been wrong.

A split-second later, it seemed to happen in slow motion when he made two steps towards the guardrail and jumped over it, down into the river. With everyone else, Ellie rushed to the place where he'd been seconds ago.

Shriver was nowhere to be seen.

If he wanted the story to have a spectacular ending, he'd certainly achieved that goal.

"You did good," Maria told her when they walked back to the car.

"Not good enough." The search wasn't over, but now they were likely looking for a body. Ellie wasn't looking forward to updating Jordan on the news.

Wondering why Derek wasn't here yet, she finally turned on her phone, her jaw dropping at the numbers of messages and missed calls—one in particular.

"Oh boy," Maria, looking over her shoulder, said. "Okay, here's what we do. I'll stay here, and I can bring the car later. Casey will drive you, that'll be faster." She waved to Officer Lyons who came sprinting over. "Emergency," she told the officer. "Harding's wife is having the baby. Get her to the hospital fast?"

Ellie felt the color drain from her face when Maria said it out loud. No two-week prep time, no relaxed baby shower. It was happening *now*.

"No problem," Casey said cheerily, taking Ellie by the arm. "Come on, let's move. This is so exciting! You must be thrilled."

Casey had children. If she said it was exciting, that was a good sign, right?

Ellie was afraid she'd miss the moment. She was afraid she wouldn't be everything Jordan needed right now, but yes, above all, she was excited, pushing the image of Shriver jumping off the bridge out of her mind.

❧

"It's a good thing you came in." The doctor said to Derek, "We'll get your wife settled in, it will just take a moment."

Jordan felt like she couldn't afford to waste any energy beyond rolling her eyes, while Derek answered, "No, I had nothing to do with this. *Her wife* is on the way."

"Oh. Sure. Okay." The young man blushed. "Mrs...Detective...You're Dr. McVey's patient? I'll get her."

"Thank you."

The sound of rapid footsteps alerted them to Ellie who came rushing towards them.

"I'm here! I'm here. What did I miss?"

"Nothing yet."

Just like that, the world righted itself, because she didn't have to change plans, give birth in the living room or in traffic. Ellie's presence was a relief.

"How did it go? Did you catch him?"

The look that passed between Ellie and Casey was concerning, but Jordan decided she had no more time to care.

"I'll tell you later," Ellie leaned down to kiss her.

"Sounds good."

❧

"You look a little shell shocked," Pauline said gently, taking Ellie's hand. "Jordan did amazing. So did you."

"I didn't really do anything." She flexed the fingers of her right hand, still slightly sensitive. Maybe that wasn't entirely true, but for sure, hers was a small contribution in comparison. She cast a glance at the room where mother and baby were asleep. Pauline had taken her outside before she and Jack would leave and come back the next morning.

"You did, and you will do a lot more than you think. Let's sit for a moment?" Ellie followed her to the chairs a few feet away, glad not to have to stay upright any longer. She felt a bit light-headed, happy, antsy, all of it at the same time. And her vision blurred every so often, for all the same reasons.

"What's on your mind?"

"Many things," Ellie said truthfully. Jordan was fine, and Meri was, so she made an effort to sort out her jumbled emotions. "We have a baby now." The sheer concept was amazing and scary. They'd go home with a tiny new human. "To be precise, Jordan had a baby. What if Meri grows up and she can't be that close to me? Jordan was sometimes worried about the kind of mother she'd be, but we already know she'll be awesome. I promised her we'd be good at this. What if I'm not?"

Pauline patiently waited until Ellie was running out of words and breath.

"I've been where you are," she said. "You are scared, and I can promise you it won't be the last time. You'll take it one day at a time, and you'll love her with everything you have—I know you already do."

"Yes. I do," Ellie whispered. She imagined how equally worried and hopeful Pauline must have been when a twelve-year-old Jordan arrived at their home.

"Jordan did a great job bringing your daughter into the world. At the same time, and she knows that, you don't have to give birth to be a mother. You'll be a great team, as you are with everything else."

Finally, Ellie could breathe again, and she didn't feel like keeling over any longer.

"Thank you so much. I have a lot to learn from you."

Pauline laughed wistfully. "Jack and I will be happy to help any way we can. I'm not perfect. I've had my moments. I thought it wasn't fair that Kathryn is now around for all the good times when she wasn't willing to do the hard parenting stuff. I had to let that go, because if it wasn't for her, we wouldn't have Jordan."

"I know what you mean." Ellie smiled, still tired, but a lot less confused. "Thank you for everything. I'll see you both in the morning."

"You will. Have a good night."

Before Ellie stole back into the room, she checked her phone, reading the message from Maria. *Congratulations. We're all happy for you.*

Even though dealing with the other subject was the last thing Ellie wanted to do at the moment, she made a quick call.

"No, we didn't find a body, and also, have you looked at the time?"

Doing so now, Ellie winced. "Wow, I'm sorry."

"That's okay. Today of all days, I forgive you. But honestly, there isn't much you or anyone can do. It's unlikely that some-one could survive this."

"Yeah. I'll try to forget about it for a while. I'll talk to you soon."

"Not too soon," Maria said softly. "Take your time."

"We will. Thank you."

Ellie turned off her phone and went back into the room, standing silently over Meri's bed, vision blurring again before she turned to Jordan, jumping a little when she realized Jordan wasn't asleep.

"She's perfect." Ellie had already said this today, but there was something she needed to add. "There are no words to describe how much I love you."

"Good. Because I love you the same."

As long as they were here together, where nothing and no one could intrude, she'd remember this perfect moment, with nothing to worry about.

They'd be awesome, just like she'd promised.

About the Author

B arbara Winkes writes sapphic crime drama and Christmas romance. She loves writing characters who get the job done, whether it's stopping a predator or saving cherished traditions—while still making time for love. She lives with her wife in Quebec City.

barbarawinkes.com

Also by Barbara Winkes

Luce Allen Mysteries
In Harm's Way
Under Pressure

The Crossing Lines Trilogy
Undercover
Redemption
Vengeance

The Connected Series
Promised to the Queen
Drawn to the Enemy
Tempted by the Protector
Saved by the Heiress

Carpenter/Harding
Indiscretions
Insinuations
Incisions
Intrusions

Initiations
Intentions
Infatuations
Impressions
Implications
Infractions
Incidents
Illusions

Kelli & Merin Romantic Suspense
Thunder
Rain

Lord and Burton
Clean Slate

Standalone
The Amnesia Project